Five Nights at Freddy's

FAZBEAR FRIGHTS #4
STEP CLOSER

BY

**SCOTT CAWTHON
ANDREA WAGGENER
ELLEY COOPER
KELLY PARRA**

Scholastic Inc.

If you purchased this book without a cover, you should be aware that this book is stolen property. It was reported as "unsold and destroyed" to the publisher, and neither the author nor the publisher has received any payment for this "stripped book."

Copyright © 2020 by Scott Cawthon. All rights reserved.

Photo of TV static: © Klikk/Dreamstime

All rights reserved. Published by Scholastic Inc., *Publishers since 1920*. SCHOLASTIC and associated logos are trademarks and/or registered trademarks of Scholastic Inc.

The publisher does not have any control over and does not assume any responsibility for author or third-party websites or their content.

No part of this publication may be reproduced, stored in a retrieval system, or transmitted in any form or by any means, electronic, mechanical, photocopying, recording, or otherwise, without written permission of the publisher. For information regarding permission, write to Scholastic Inc., Attention: Permissions Department, 557 Broadway, New York, NY 10012.

This book is a work of fiction. Names, characters, places, and incidents are either the product of the author's imagination or are used fictitiously, and any resemblance to actual persons, living or dead, business establishments, events, or locales is entirely coincidental.

Library of Congress Cataloging-in-Publication Data available

ISBN 978-1-338-57605-4

10 9 8 7 6 5   22 23 24

Printed in the U.S.A.

First printing 2020 • Book design by Betsy Peterschmidt

TABLE OF CONTENTS

```
Step Closer. . . . . . . 1
Dance with Me. . . . .  77
Coming Home. . . . . 131
```

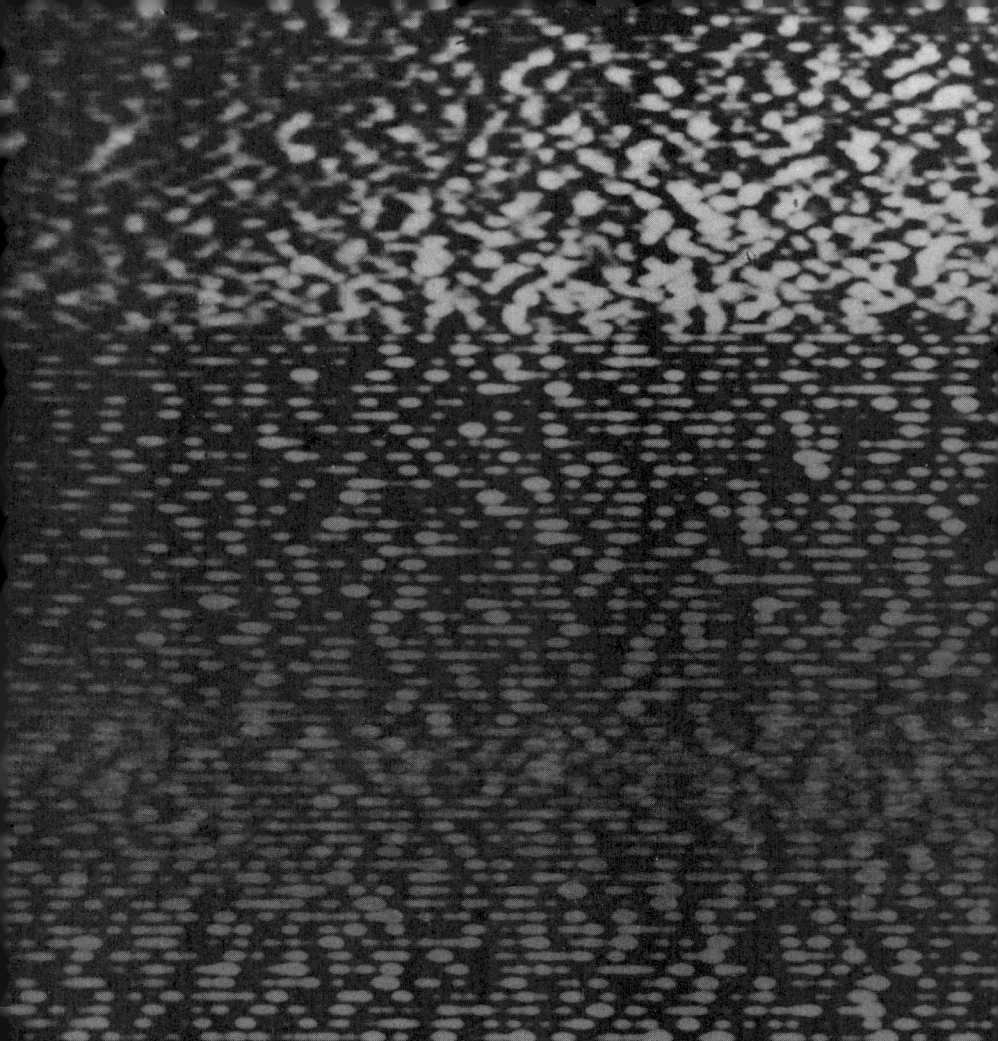

STEP CLOSER

Foxy's yellow eyes glowed in the darkness of the room. His jaw hung open, flashing sharp teeth. Foxy lifted his hook and slashed its sharp tip in front of Pete's face, the hook whizzing by his nose. Pete rolled off the bed, his body shaking. His stomach pitched as he lay helpless on the floor and Foxy pivoted, looming over him. The shifting of gears filled the room as Foxy swung up with his hook.

"You can be a pirate, but first you'll have to lose an eye and an arm."

"No," Pete breathed.

When Foxy slammed his hook down into Pete's eye, an audible pop sounded. Blood poured from his eye socket as Pete screamed . . .

Freddy Fazbear's Pizza was crowded with crazy little kids and their harassed idiot parents. Music bellowed through wall speakers, and arcade games pinged and vibrated. The scent of burnt pepperoni wafted through the air, mixed with the scent of cotton candy. Pete was slouched against a wall, ankles crossed and ball cap turned backward, drinking a cherry-flavored cola while chewing watermelon gum. His little brother and his friends were crowded around an arcade game.

Pete didn't want to be there, but his mother had to work and Chuck *had* to be with his friends after school again. So that left Pete to play babysitter. For the hundredth time, he asked himself, why was it always *his* job? And was the little snot grateful?

Nope.

Chuck was always whining about his inhaler. Always whining he was hungry. Always asking a bunch of questions. Always something. Since their dad had left, Pete was saddled with everything Chuck.

His mom's words were stuck in his head. *You're the man of the house now, Pete. Take care of your little brother.*

How was Pete supposed to be the man when he was just sixteen? Did anyone ask him what he thought of his new responsibilities?

Double nope.

Pete watched a little kid walk up to a couple of employees cleaning up birthday tables. He pulled on a guy's sleeve. The man looked down at the kid and smiled. "Can I help you with something?" he asked.

"I was wondering, where is Foxy the Pirate?" the kid said.

The man's voice was syrupy sweet. "Oh, Foxy's on vacation at the moment. We hope to have him back soon."

The little kid stuck his lip out, but nodded as he walked away.

The other employee chuckled. "Good one," he told the man.

"Yeah, on vacation in the maintenance room. Don't know when they'll bring the show out again."

Pete was thinking that over when he realized someone was saying his name. "Pete?"

He pulled his attention from the conversation and moved his gaze toward Maria Rodriguez, who was standing beside him. Her black hair brushed her shoulders and her lips were glossy red. She had these bright green eyes with long lashes and a few freckles on her nose. She was a cheerleader at their high school and he'd known her since the sixth grade. So why did he suddenly feel so nervous around her?

"Hey, Maria," he said.

"Stuck here with little Chuckie, huh?"

Pete scowled. "Yeah."

"Same here. My little sister's birthday." Maria motioned to a birthday table in front of the stage, with little kids wearing cone hats and eating cake. "Can't believe we used to be like them."

He smirked. "Don't know about you, but I was never like that."

Maria smiled. "*Sure*. So, where you been? Haven't seen you at practice lately."

He'd been benched from football for unnecessary roughness and having a bad attitude on multiple occasions. Hello? This was football! So he'd just quit altogether. The truth was, Pete never used to quit anything. He used to finish whatever he started. But after seeing his parents quit each other, finishing things didn't matter so much anymore. Plus, he didn't need any more grief from the coach—he got enough of that from his teachers and his mom. A kid could only handle so much griping.

He shrugged. "Got tired of it all, you know?"

"Yeah, I guess. So, what are you going to do with all your free time now?"

"Well . . ."

Someone waved to Maria from the party table and her face lit up. "Yes! Finally time to leave." Before she left, she added, "Hey, a bunch of us are meeting under old Beacon Bridge if you want to come to hang out later."

Pete smiled. "Yeah?"

She nodded. "It'll be fun."

Then he shook his head. "Can't. I have to watch Chuck the Chump."

"Oh, okay. Maybe next time. See ya around school."

Irritation washed over Pete as he watched Maria walk away. This was all Chuck's fault. Little brat. Everything was always about his little brother. Didn't matter what Pete wanted because *nothing* mattered when it came to Pete. Dad had left. Mom was in her own little world. They figured they'd just put Pete in charge of Chuck because they didn't have the time to deal with him themselves. But Pete had never signed up to take over their responsibilities. He was a kid and kids should be free, not worrying about stuff. They should be able to do what they wanted, like hanging out with other kids instead of watching little brothers. But his parents didn't care about any of that, obviously. After all, they never asked Pete if he had wanted them to split up in the first place. They just divorced, and that was that. None of it was fair.

Pete had so many emotions inside of him that sometimes he just didn't know what to do with them. Sometimes he felt like a ticking bomb about to explode, like the tension in his body was just under his skin, begging for release. For a while, football had helped. He'd been a beast on the field, taking down players, throwing people out of the way. By the end of practice, he'd been exhausted and empty. Empty was better. It was good. But since he was off the team, Pete was stuck without an outlet. He hated these feelings. He hated *everything* sometimes. He watched his brother break off from his friends to head to the bathroom and his eyes narrowed on the fresh opportunity. Pete tossed his soda at an empty table and walked quickly to his brother's side, latching on to his arm forcefully.

Chuck's face screwed up. "Ow, Pete!"

"Shut up and walk," he muttered, then blew a bubble till it popped.

"Why? Where are we going?"

"You'll see." With a quick look over his shoulder, Pete hustled his little brother down a long and darkened corridor. The floor was faded and old, and peeling posters of animatronics lined the walls. The place needed a serious upgrade. Pete had wandered down here before and discovered the large maintenance room. Now that he knew what was taking a vacation inside, he couldn't wait to take Chuck along for a little adventure, considering his brother had always been scared of a certain animatronic.

Chuck started to protest. "Where are we going?"

"What's the matter, you scared?"

"No! I just want to stay with my friends!"

"We're going to check something out."

Chuck hiccupped and licked his dry lips around his braces. He sounded like a toad when he was nervous. "Just leave me alone or I'm telling Mom."

"You're such a little snitch. Now you're really going in."

Pete dragged his surprisingly strong little brother

through the entrance of the maintenance room to meet Foxy the Pirate.

The heavy door slammed behind them engulfing them in darkness.

"Pete, let me go!"

"*Quiet*. Someone might hear and I don't want to listen to you whining like a baby. Do you know how annoying that is?" Pete wouldn't let loose of the vise grip he had on his brother. No, it was time to teach Chuck a lesson. It was time for Pete to do what he wanted and right now that meant giving his brother a good scare.

Little Chuck the Chump might even pee his pants.

Pete chuckled at the idea.

With one hand still firmly on his brother's arm, he fished his phone out of his pocket and turned on the light to guide them slowly through the darkness. The area was strangely quiet, as if it wasn't connected to a boatload of people just down a hallway. The smell here was stagnant and musty, and the air seemed . . . lifeless. As if no one had set foot in the place recently. Which was weird when the rest of the building was full of activity.

"*Hiccup*."

Pete's foot knocked a bottle across the floor. It hit something and shattered. Pete and Chuck froze, wondering if someone would hear, but no one seemed to be around.

"*Hiccup*."

Pete scanned the floor with the light, revealing scuffed

black-and-white checkered tiles. Dusty tables and a few broken chairs were scattered about the large room. There were cardboard boxes on the tables, half empty with party hats and plates scattered around them. His light flashed on a big, black spider sitting on the edge of one box.

"Aw, look at that sucker. It's huge!" Pete said.

The spider jumped away and the boys leaped back.

"*I hate spiders*. Let's get out of here," Chuck whined again.

"Not yet. There's so much more to explore. Think of it like one of those adventure games you like to play. We have to find the secret treasure." Pete said, laughing under his breath. More like he had to scare the crap out of his brother a little more.

He flashed the light back down to the floor. He stopped on what looked like dark melted candles and strange, black markings.

"What is that? Are those symbols?" Chuck wanted to know.

"Who cares." Pete continued to wave the light around. Then he saw the small stage with the closed purple curtain, and a grin split his mouth. Pinned to the curtain, there was a crooked sign with the words OUT OF SERVICE.

"Score. Hopefully, it still works."

"*Hiccup*. Pete . . . we shouldn't be here. We could get in trouble. Like *big* trouble. Like trespassing, you know? That's against the law."

"*That's against the law*," Pete mimicked him in a tiny

voice. "You're such a nerd, you know that? What are you going to be when you grow up, Chuck? A cop? I'll be sure to buy you a donut on the way home."

Pete shined the light next to the stage, revealing a rusted control box on a side table. The cover was broken off the box.

"This is going to be so good." He dragged his brother to the foot of the stage. "Enjoy the show, little brother."

"Stop it, Pete!"

He grabbed Chuck by the shirt and pants, giving him a good wedgie as he launched him onto the little stage. Chuck crashed onto the platform with an "ugh," and Pete rushed to the control box.

He slammed a palm on a button that said START. Again, and then again. A low hum sounded, followed by a muffled click and clank.

"Aw, come on!" Pete yelled when nothing happened.

Finally, the small curtain began to open.

"Hiccup—hiccup—hiccup."

In a quick motion, Chuck rolled to the side.

"Chuck, you wimp!" Pete rushed to the stage, grabbing Chuck by his sneakers to keep him there. In the quick moves only fear can bring on, Chuck managed to evade his brother. He climbed to his feet, jumped off the platform, and ran.

That was the fastest Pete had ever seen his brother run. If he hadn't been running from Pete, he might even be impressed. Pete moved to get him back, then came to halt in front of the stage as his shirt caught on something.

"Dang," he muttered. He tugged on his shirt, but it was caught on a stupid nail.

Choppy music sounded through the air as the curtains opened fully. Pete stood frozen in front of a fractured Foxy animatronic that was glaring down at him. The yellow eyes glowed under red brows, and an eye patch flipped up over his right eye. A jaw with sharp, pointy teeth hung loosely as the big fox began to sing a disjointed song about becoming a pirate. One arm had a hook for a hand and the other hand was stripped of fur, showing its robotic skeleton. Strange sounds of whirling gears screeched and seemed to echo in the quiet of the room. The robot's chest appeared ripped open, exposing more of his mechanical body. Foxy moved slowly, eerily. Even though Pete knew he was a robot, his deteriorated body looked to be half-eaten away by who knew what.

A shiver skittered down Pete's spine.

He swallowed his gum.

He couldn't move his gaze away from Foxy's yellow eyes as he sang.

Didn't know why . . . just a dumb, old robot . . .

"You can be a pirate, but first you'll have to lose an eye and an arm! Yarg! —first you'll have to lose an eye and an arm! Yarg! —first you'll have to lose an eye and an arm! Yarg! —first you'll have to lose an eye and an arm! Yarg!"

The old animatronic was stuck on the same lyric . . .

"—first you'll have to lose an eye and an arm! Yarg!"

Pete blinked as a strange feeling came over him like an invisible cold, heavy blanket was covering every inch of his body, then sinking through his skin and into his bones.

"*—first you'll have to lose an eye and an arm! Yarg!*"

The room grew still with a sudden silence, yet Pete remained standing there in the dark. Unmoving.

He blinked and looked around, trying to remember where he was. He was in the dark. Alone. His pulse scrambled as he stepped back. Then he saw his shirt was caught on a nail, and it all came back to him. He rubbed at his eyes, yanked his shirt from the nail, and stormed away from the stage to find his brother.

"Dang it, Chuck!"

Pete watched Chuck suck in a puff of his inhaler before he sat down at the dinner table. He could tell his little brother's nerves were still shot from when Pete took him to see Foxy the Pirate. Chuck eyed Pete across the table and squirmed. Pete didn't know what he was so upset about. The little brat didn't even get to see the best part of the show. He'd run away and stuck closely to his friends until it was time to come home.

"How was Freddy Fazbear's Pizza, boys?" their mom asked as she set plates of ham and potatoes in front of them.

"Fine," Chuck said, without looking up from his plate.

"Yeah, just dandy," Pete muttered, swallowing mashed potatoes.

"What? Did something happen?"

"No, nothing," the brothers said together.

Pete gave Chuck a warning look. *Better not tell . . .*

Mom raised her eyebrows as she sat down. "Okay. Well, I have something exciting to share with you both. I thought it was time for us to do something as a family. And something that was good for the world."

Pete bit back words that would likely hurt his mom's feelings. *What family?* It had been nearly six months since Dad had left and broken up their family. And when had she become a do-gooder?

"Something new. Something that represents a fresh start for the three of us as a family unit. Something that could give someone else a fresh start, too." She pulled out a paper from a folder and turned it toward them.

Pete read the bold letters in disbelief. "Organ donors?"

Mom nodded in excitement. "Yes, we'll be family donors. Doesn't that sound great?"

Chuck's gaze met Pete's in astonishment.

"This is your exciting news? You really want us to give up our body parts?" Pete asked her.

She waved her hand at Pete. "Only if something happens to us, silly! Which obviously we don't want. But if it did, we could actually help other people who are sick and in need of a new heart or a kidney. We could save someone's life. We'd be heroes."

"We'd be dead heroes," Chuck said.

She laughed. "Oh, Chuckles, you make me laugh!"

"Yeah, *Chuckles*, you're a riot," Pete said, deadpan.

Chuck scrunched up his face. "Hey, Mom, you know what Pete did at the pizza place?"

Pete narrowed his eyes at Chuck. He knew the little brat couldn't keep his mouth shut.

"What did he do?"

"He drank *way* too much soda." Chuck smiled, flashing his railroad tracks.

Mom sighed. "Pete, come on. I told you what all that soda does to your teeth."

Pete just looked back at his mom. What was with her lately? Last month she'd started to see someone who called herself a "life coach." Then his mom had started yoga, chopped her long hair off, and gone on some weird juice cleanse. She'd also gathered a bunch of their stuff and given it away to charity. Now . . . she wanted to donate their *body parts*?

"Here, read the flyer, Pete," Mom said. "It'll convince you, for sure."

Pete grabbed the paper his mom shoved under his nose. The list of organ donations was pretty long: Bones, heart, kidney, liver, pancreas, skin, intestine, eyeballs . . .

Eyeballs.

You can be a pirate, but first you'll have to lose an eye and an arm! Yarg!

Pete flashed back to Foxy. He imagined Foxy suddenly walking off the stage and stalking toward him with his big, sharp hook. His mechanical feet scraping across the floor.

Pete's mashed potatoes did a slow roll in his stomach,

and he suddenly felt light-headed. He blinked the image away. "What a dumb idea, Mom."

"Pete, it's not dumb. And it hurts my feelings that you think that."

Yeah, Mom was into expressing her feelings lately, too. He shoved his chair away from the table and stood up as his face flashed cold, then hot. "I'm not doing it, Mom."

"*Pete.*"

"I don't want to talk about it. I'm going to bed." Pete walked out of the dining room.

"What happened?" he heard his mom ask.

Chuck sighed. "Puberty."

"Hurry up, Pete!"

The next morning, Chuck banged on the bathroom door. If Pete didn't get out soon, Chuck would be late for the bus to W. H. Jameson Middle School. If he missed the bus, then he'd have to ride his bike five miles to school and his mom would freak out over his going alone. She was paranoid something would happen if Pete wasn't with him, which he didn't understand, since he was almost twelve! (Well, eleven and a half.) Lots of his friends were left by themselves all the time, but not Chuck. Pete always said it was because Chuck was the baby and their mom couldn't stop thinking of him that way.

He heard Pete heave into the toilet and Chuck stepped back and cringed. Pete was sick, he figured. Chuck's lip curled a little. *That's what he deserves for trying to scare me yesterday.* Then he let that thought go as Pete heaved again, stepping back and leaning against the wall to wait. Chuck knew Dad's leaving had changed everyone. Pete was angry all the time. Mom kept searching for new things to make her happy. As for himself? He just tried to keep busy. He liked to hang out with his friends, he liked to play online video games, and he was pretty interested in puzzles.

Yeah, middle school sucked, but going to school was just a part of life you had to get through. Every once in a while, he felt challenged by a project, then he'd complete it and get bored again until something else caught his interest. He got why Pete hated him half the time, because Mom made Pete watch over him so much. He tried not to be annoying. But everything that came out of his mouth seemed to annoy Pete. Maybe it was just like that with all brothers? Chuck didn't know because he didn't have another brother to compare to.

The toilet flushed. A minute later, Pete swung open the door. A wave of serious stink wafted at Chuck and he waved a hand in front of his nose. Pete didn't look so good. His face was so pale his freckles stood out like tiny bugs on his cheeks. His dark hair stuck up in different directions like he'd jammed his finger in a socket and shocked himself, and there were dark circles under his eyes.

"Geez, Pete, what's the matter with you?"

"Nothing," Pete spat out. "Something didn't agree with me. Probably something from that stupid Freddy Fazbear's Pizza."

Chuck didn't think so. "Do you want me to call Mom?"

Pete shoved him aside. "No, I'm not a little baby like you, Chuck the Chump."

Chuck felt his shoulders stiffen. He hated that stupid nickname. "Whatever," he mumbled. He slammed and locked the bathroom door behind him.

Pete chugged an energy drink with triple caffeine while running to his bio class, but he still felt drained and exhausted. He'd had some pretty crazy dreams last night. He couldn't remember much, only that there had been all this blood. It was everywhere, pouring all over him, down his face and over his chest and arms. When he'd jerked awake, his blankets were tangled around his body. He'd fallen to the floor trying to unwind the blankets just so he could rush to the bathroom to blow chunks.

He shivered just thinking about it, but he rolled his shoulders and shoved that not-so-fun memory away. He probably should have stayed home, but calling his mom at work would have freaked her out and she'd be asking him a million questions. He'd decided just to get through the day somehow. He loped into his classroom five minutes after the bell.

"Mr. Dinglewood, you are late," droned Mr. Watson in a bored voice. "Note?"

Pete snatched off his hat and shook his head in a negative. He took an empty stool at the workstation in the far back, next to a kid in a black leather jacket and purple hair.

Pete zipped his hat into his pack and set it on the floor, then wiped some sweat off his forehead. He shifted awkwardly on the stool. Why couldn't he seem to keep still?

"As I was saying, class, we will be dissecting a frog today," said Mr. Watson. "You have all been quizzed on the safety rules for the tools and procedure. You will work as a team with your partner to fill out the lab sheet. I expect you all to be mature young people. I know that will be hard for some of you, but there is no funny business here or you will fail. You do not want to fail. You have thirty minutes starting now."

When they both turned toward the dead frog sprawled out in front of them, Leather Jacket Guy leaned forward. "Dude . . . what's the matter with you?"

Pete shook his head. "Nothing."

Leather Jacket Guy gave him a *yeah, right* look and picked up a small scalpel.

Ten minutes in, Pete yawned. His mouth was dry and his hand was starting to shake from the precise cutting.

Leather Jacket Guy smirked. "Hey, check this out," he said, and poked the frog in its eye with the scalpel. A weird liquid gushed out. "Sick, right?" Then he shoved the blade into the frog's arm and sliced it off. He picked up the tiny hand and waved it at Pete.

Pete shook his head. "I need a break."

"Look, I'm sorry. I swear I'll stop messing around." He held out the little frog hand. "Here, let's shake on it."

The kid chuckled as Pete pushed off the stool and headed

for the classroom water fountain. He took a long couple of drinks. Dang, he was thirsty. And he was starving! His stomach decided to growl then, since he'd skipped breakfast trying to make it to school on time.

He was heading back to his workstation when Mr. Watson stopped him. "Everything going well, Mr. Dinglewood?" he asked.

Mr. Watson was shorter than him, with white hair and a white mustache. Glasses hung on the tip of his red nose, as if somehow he was looking down on Pete—even though that was physically impossible.

"Yep, things are fine," Pete blurted.

Mr. Watson frowned. "Glad to hear it. Now, please return to your dissection lab. You of all people cannot afford to fail."

"That's what I'm doing," Pete muttered, whirling around.

It all went downhill from there.

Pete took a quick, long stride and his foot landed on his pack strap instead of landing securely on the floor. That was when he slipped, losing his footing, falling backward. He felt his toe connect with Leather Jacket Guy in a brutal way. The kid yelped, and Mr. Watson shouted something in reply.

Pete landed on his back, his breath knocked out of him. He blinked, and when he opened his eyes he spotted the kid's scalpel in the air. The small knife must have flown up on impact. But then, in disbelief, Pete saw the scalpel lose gravity and fall toward his face, the point of the tiny blade coming straight for his eye.

Adrenaline spurted through his body. With the quick reflexes that came from years of playing football, Pete swatted the tool away like a deadly insect just as the blade was about to blind him. The scalpel hit the stand of the workstation and fell to the floor.

"Holy . . ." Leather Jacket Guy hissed.

"Dear Lord, Peter, are you all right?" said Mr. Watson, hovering over him like a frightened parent. "Don't move, I'll call the nurse. Class, stay seated! Nobody move! Emergency procedure, please! Out of the way!"

The class ignored Mr. Watson and crowded around Pete as his chest rose up and down with heavy breaths. He didn't think he'd hit his head, but he felt dizzy and kind of out of it. Not to mention mortified.

Someone whispered, "Way to go, Dingleberry."

A couple of kids giggled. "Yeah, what a loser. Now we know why he was kicked off the football team."

Pete slowly sat up as his face flushed red. Dang, there was no doubt he should have stayed home.

Somehow, Pete managed to get through the rest of the school day. The nurse had checked him out and given him an ice pack and sent him on his way. It was a relief when the final bell rang and he walked quickly around slow-moving kids, through the doors, and down the school's front steps. When he checked his phone, he saw he had a new text from his mother. He rubbed a hand over his face.

What now? Couldn't he get through one day without her asking him to do something? Yeah, he loved his mom but now that she didn't have his dad to help her, Pete was always on call. She better not ask him to take Chuck out again. He wouldn't do it. He'd say "Nope, sorry, I'm sick." He clicked on the text:

Hi Pete, after school could you swing by the butcher and pick up my order of pork chops?

He responded flatly: **Fine.**

She responded: **Thank you!** (Heart emoji).

Pete popped a wad of watermelon gum into his mouth and set off walking to the butcher shop, which was a couple of blocks out of his way. He wanted to get his license, and that was the plan six months ago, before the divorce, but now everyone seemed to have forgotten.

He finally arrived at Barney's Butcher Shop during a lull. No cars were parked in front, which was perfect, because he could get the order and get out fast. Pete pushed through the glass door, and no one was even behind the counter. Sale prices were posted on the glass and some old rock music was playing from the back.

He walked to the display case of raw meats, scanning left, then right.

"Hello?" he called out. "Yo, I got an order to pick up."

There wasn't a bell to ring, so he stood around for another minute waiting for someone to help him. When no one came, he'd about had it. He knocked on the glass counter a couple of times. "Hellloooo!"

Finally, he took matters into his own hands, walking behind the tall display case. "Hey, anyone here or what?"

On the other side of the case was a long butcher table with watery, red liquid on it. The overpowering scent of meat and blood made his guts swish around again. The gum in his mouth turned sour. He put a hand to his stomach as if to ease it. *I will not blow chunks. I will not blow chunks,* he thought. He looked around to distract himself, but all he saw were pictures of butchered animals. When he craned his head in another direction, he was surrounded by rows of lethal-looking knives and cleavers hanging above his head. A new wave of dizziness washed over him. He set his hand out for balance on the butcher table, felt the watery liquid on his fingertips, and broke out in a cold sweat.

Wham.

A huge meat cleaver slammed down into the wood, barely missing his wrist. Pete shot backward, protecting his hand against his chest, knocking into the display case with his pack. He gazed at the meat cleaver embedded in the wood. The handle vibrated in the air as if the force had been incredibly strong. His gaze whipped up toward the hanging tools.

One empty hook was swaying slowly. The meat cleaver had fallen from the hook. *Fallen?* He didn't think something could fall so forcefully on its own, but what else could have happened?

"Hey, what are you doing back here?" A stocky, older man wearing a bloody apron waddled into the area, wiping his hands with a towel. "Employees only. Can't you read the signs?"

Pete pointed to the cleaver stuck in the butcher table. "I-I—"

"Ah, nah. You can't be playing with my knives. You trying to get me in trouble, kid? Health department will have my license."

"I-I . . ."

"Spit it out. What's the matter?"

"I didn't touch anything. It-it just fell."

The old man narrowed his eyes. "No way these knives fall from those hooks, kid. If that were the case, I'd be missing a lot more fingers than the ones I already cut off." The old man raised his left hand to show a missing pinky and a ring finger with its top lopped off. The skin looked smooth on the two oddly shaped finger stumps.

When Pete started to shake, the man laughed. "Scared? Never seen someone with missing fingers before? Well, keep your fingers and hands away from sharp objects, kid, and you should be just fine. *Maybe.*" He cracked up again.

Pete swallowed hard. "Just here . . . to pick up an order for . . . Dinglewood."

The butcher waved a hand toward the back room. "Yeah, got that in the fridge. Chops, right? I'll be right with you."

Pete whipped open the front door to his house and slammed it as soon as he'd stormed through. He tossed his pack on the floor and strode to the kitchen, where he opened the fridge, threw the chops in, and grabbed a soda. He shut the door with his hip and chugged the whole can. The cola soothed his throat and the sweetness calmed him a little.

What a freaky day.

He took off his cap and ran his hand over his head. He just needed to eat, rest, and forget about everything else. No more crazy dreams, or weird kids with scalpels, and definitely no more butcher shops. His mom was going to have to pick up the meat herself from now on. He glanced out the kitchen window when he heard the backyard gate creak open. Chuck pushed his bike in and leaned it on the side of the house before coming through the side door.

Pete felt his irritation bubble up. "Are you crazy?" he asked Chuck. "If Mom finds out you biked to school—"

"*Someone* hogged the bathroom this morning and I was late for the bus."

"—And I didn't pick you up, I'm busted."

"I won't tell."

"Yeah right! You always snitch."

Chuck rolled his eyes. "I didn't tell her about you forcing me into the maintenance room, did I?"

"Not yet. But I saw how you wanted to tell her last night at dinner. You thought you were real funny."

Chuck held up his hands in exasperation. "Well, I didn't! That has to count for something."

Pete shrugged. "Still, you can't be trusted."

"Fine, I should just tell her to get you busted!! How 'bout that?"

"See? You *are* a snitch!"

"Shut up, you are!"

"You shut up, you little twerp!"

Chuck gave in. "Whatever, jerkwad," he muttered. He grabbed a loaf of bread from the bread box, then the peanut butter from the pantry, then the jelly from the fridge. He pulled a butter knife from the drawer and started to make himself a sandwich.

When he saw Pete eyeing his sandwich, he lifted his eyebrows. "What? You want one?"

Pete hesitated. "Don't know."

"Well, make your own."

Pete held a hand to his stomach, debating if he could handle it.

"You still sick or something?" Chuck wanted to know.

He shrugged. "Just an off day."

"Why, what happened?"

Pete snapped, "Don't worry about it. None of your business." No freaking way would he tell anyone else about the embarrassing incident in bio class and the flying cleavers. Especially not his twerp brother who would run and tell Mom and freak her out.

"Fine." Chuck finished making the sandwich and slid it across the counter toward Pete. A peace offering?

Pete lifted his eyebrows in surprise as Chuck began making another.

"You know Mom filled out that organ donor paperwork for us," Chuck said, like it was casual conversation.

Pete's jaw dropped. "What? Why?"

Chuck nodded, flashing his braces, looking almost pleased. "She said you'd come around to the idea eventually."

"But I told her not to!"

"Since when does Mom ever listen to what we want?" Chuck took a bite of his sandwich and kept talking with his mouth full. "It's not a big deal, anyway. You're dead when they take your organs. Your life or soul or whatever is gone. What do I care? Why do *you* even care so much?"

Pete didn't even know where to start. Here he was, trying to save his body parts all day long, and his mom was trying to give them away! "It's—it's just a stupid idea!"

Chuck gave him a curious look. "Wait. You're scared, aren't you?"

"No, shut up!"

"I looked it up. You want to know how they cut into you and take your organs? It's so cool! They split you open, like in a 'Y' incision, then your guts are all hanging out. Then they remove everything piece by piece." He made a face, with his eyes rolled back and his tongue hanging out. "Your intestines are super long, right? So they just pull them out like a long rope of link sausage." Chuck made a motion with his hands like he was pulling out a long piece of rope from his stomach.

"I said to shut up!" Pete grabbed the sandwich and fled to his room.

The next morning, Pete sipped from his triple caffeine energy drink as he walked to school. The sun was out, which improved the walk a lot. Today had to be better than yesterday, he figured. Last night he had weird dreams again, but luckily the details drifted away as soon as he woke up. And there hadn't been any spewing his guts into the toilet, so that was a score.

He'd barely spoken to his mom last night or this morning. Why had she signed him up as a donor when he'd told her not to? He didn't even want to eat the pork chops he'd picked up last night; all they did was remind him that he'd nearly lost his hand.

When he passed a construction site, he paused a moment. He looked across the street and decided against crossing with all the busy traffic—instead, he'd go right under the scaffolding. Pete scanned the boards above him, making sure there weren't any weird tools that could fall on his head. He heard motorized saws and drills sounding from inside the site but nothing coming from the scaffolding. When he figured he was safe, he relaxed a little.

Just in case, he walked cautiously under the boards, with quick glances above him. One thing he'd learned recently was that he couldn't be too careful. As he neared the end of the scaffolding, he took a breath of relief.

Piece of cake.

From inside the site, he heard a funny buzz and then a harsh clank. The hairs on Pete's arms stood up.

"What the hell—*watch out!*" someone shouted.

Pete spotted something moving fast in his peripheral vision. His head turned in time to see a circular buzz saw blade flying in his direction, reminding him of a flying Frisbee with sharp teeth.

His jaw went slack. His adrenaline spiked. He dove backward as the round blade flew through the air toward him. He held up his hand in defense, like maybe he could catch it, then he realized that was the worst thing to do and tried to pull his hand out of the path of the flying blade. He thought he was home free when he felt it slice into his flesh just above his wrist, followed by a sharp stinging.

He crashed to the ground, his drink pouring over him. Air gushed out of his lungs. His eyes were wide as he lifted his arm, watching in shock as blood poured down his skin.

"Oh man, kid! Someone call 911!" A construction worker rushed to his side, grabbing on to his helmet as if not sure what to do with his hands. "Let me get a clean rag. Just don't move!" The worker ran off, and other people started to gather around.

"Kid, are you okay?" A man in a suit stood above Pete and leaned down. He had a phone to his ear. "Hello, yeah. There's been an accident. There's a teenager—he's bleeding. On the arm. Uh, at a construction site on Willington and Salisbury. Hurry, please . . . don't worry, kid, help is on the way. Yes, he is conscious . . ."

Dazed, Pete glanced at the open gash on his arm. It wasn't very deep.

But . . .

He could have died.

"Pete!" Mom yelled as soon as she stepped into the house. "Pete!"

"In my room," he called out. He was lying on his bed, staring at the ceiling. After the paramedic bandaged him up at the construction site, he called his mom and walked back home. He didn't even want to wait for a ride—he wanted to get as far away from the construction site as possible. Now his energy was spent. He'd noticed his back was sore, so he'd gone to the bathroom and lifted his shirt in front of the mirror. As if his sliced arm wasn't bad enough, he also had a bunch of fresh scratches on his back from falling on the sidewalk.

Yesterday, he'd had a couple of close calls, but this latest accident was more dangerous. This time there was actual blood.

Mom swept into his bedroom in a flurry of nerves. "Oh my gosh! Oh my baby!"

Pete sighed. "Mom, I'm okay. It's a small wound. I didn't need stitches. Everything is fine."

She grabbed his hand, scanning the bandage on his arm. "How did this happen?" She felt his cheek, ran a hand over his head, and gave him a kiss on his forehead.

Pete looked at his arm and answered honestly. "Don't know, really."

Her eyes went wide. "What do you mean, you don't know? Were you not paying attention? Was the construction worker being negligent? Do we need to call a lawyer? Maybe we *should* go to the hospital."

"No. Okay, Mom? Just relax. Geez." While it was kind of nice to have all of her attention for once, her anxiety put him on edge.

"No, I am not relaxing. You could have really gotten hurt." She straightened and crossed her arms with a determined look on her face. "That's it. You are *not* walking to school anymore. You can ride a bus or get a ride. Maybe I can change my schedule. I'll drive you and your brother to school. I think I can make it all work." Then she placed her hands on her hips as if she was suddenly Wonder Woman and there was nothing that could stop her. "I *will* make it work."

"Mom, stop. It was just a . . . freak accident." Which he'd been having a lot of lately.

There was a knock at the front door before it swung open.

Pete shot up in his bed, startled. "Who the hell is that?"

"Pete, your language."

"Hello, anybody home?" bellowed a familiar voice.

Pete stared at his mom accusingly. "You called *Dad*?"

She said "Of course I called your father. Over here, Bill. In Pete's room." Quickly, she started to pick up dirty clothes that were thrown on the floor. "I have to call him when there's an emergency. Gosh, Pete, this room is a mess."

Like that was anything new.

Dad filled the doorway, wearing cargo pants and a T-shirt, with his pocket vest and a floppy canvas hat.

There was a forced smile buried under his scruffy beard. "There's my boy."

"You were fishing?" Mom asked him, surprised.

"No, not yet. I took the rest of the day off. Making it an early weekend. I'm here to take my firstborn with me to the lake. How you doing there, Pete? Let's see that arm." His dad stepped toward the bed, kicking water bottles as he went. His jaw hardened, but he didn't say anything about the mess.

Pete raised his arm for his dad's inspection, unsure what to make of his visit. He hadn't seen his dad in a couple of months. Only talked to him on the phone a few times. Suddenly he was home, like *really* home. He hadn't been inside the house in nearly six months. It used to be so normal to have Mom and Dad home together and now . . . it felt super awkward.

Dad made a *humph* sound. "Doesn't look too bad. You'll be good as new before you know it."

"Um, yeah, well. I don't think I'm up to fishing today, Dad." In fact, he *knew* he wasn't up to it. He was sore and he wanted to lay down and go to sleep. Pete gave his mom a pleading look. *Help me.*

She hesitated. "He's tired, Bill. Maybe another time. It's been a crazy morning."

Dad waved a hand. "Nonsense. He's fine. Fishing calms the nerves and relaxes the mind. Come on now, get ready to go, Pete. I got sandwiches already packed. It's going to be a great time, you'll see."

The sun was brutal even through a haze of clouds. Pete leaned back in a folding chair next to his dad on an old pier. A cooler sat between them and an old tackle box was spread open at his dad's feet. Pete's arm was sore, so he didn't do much casting of the fishing line. Instead, he took in the scene. A handful of small boats were in the lake with people—mostly old people—fishing in them. Every few minutes, the water rippled in the stiff breeze and brought with it the scent of decaying fish and plants. Pete couldn't remember his dad catching any fish at the local lake. He wondered if anyone caught anything here—ever.

It seemed weird, fishing alone with his dad. It had probably been a couple of years since they'd been to the lake, and Chuck was usually tagging along, filling the silence with a bunch of questions for Dad. Chuck always had to *know* things. Why something worked or how it worked or where things were made. Pete wasn't sure if Chuck really wanted the answers or the attention, but either way he was used to it. Chuck liked to ask questions and Pete didn't care to talk much.

"So, Pete, I want to know how you're doing," Dad said.

Pete lifted his hat, scratched his head, and slipped his cap back on. "I'm fine, Dad."

"Your mother says you stopped playing football and haven't been getting along much with your brother." His dad didn't use an accusing tone, but Pete could feel his disapproval, just like he had with his messy room. His dad always acted like it was Pete's fault when things went the wrong way. Outside events—like, say, parental actions—didn't come into the equation. *It must be cool to be an adult and be right all the time,* Pete thought.

Pete shrugged even though his dad wasn't looking at him. "I'm done with football. It's not for me anymore." The breeze blew and someone's fishing line flew past Pete's face. He flinched and looked at a guy floating in his boat a couple of yards away, paying no attention to where he was casting his line.

His dad said "All right. That's your choice, about football. But you're Chuck's big brother, and there's no choice in that."

Pete didn't exactly need to be reminded, but his dad went on.

"And as a big brother, you have some responsibility. I was a big brother to your aunt Lucy. Still am when she needs me. She's got a husband now, so she doesn't depend on me much anymore . . ." At the topic of husband, he seemed to get a little uncomfortable.

Pete ground his teeth together. Too bad he forgot his gum. Lectures were always boring and a waste of airspace, but at least gum would have been a distraction. He stared out across the lake, hoping something might break up this uncomfortable moment.

"But anyway . . . sometimes responsibility can be a lot for a kid," his dad said, clearing his throat. "You know, with school, grades, and girls making you feel funny." His dad gave him a side glance. "Got any questions about girls?"

Pete's cheeks burned and he shook his head adamantly in a negative.

"Okay, well, my point is if you need to talk to someone, I'm here for you, son." His dad turned to him fully then, staring like he was waiting for Pete to say something big.

Pete frowned. "Uh, okay."

His dad ran a hand down his beard. "Or if it's easier to talk to a stranger, I can find you a counselor."

"What? No, I don't need a counselor."

"Well, with your wrist . . ." His eyes went to Pete's bandage.

"What about it? It was an accident."

His dad's gaze became more intense. "Was it really, Pete?"

Pete jerked back. "You think I did this to myself?"

"I've heard divorce can affect families in different ways—"

"*I didn't hurt myself, Dad. Geez.*" Pete scrubbed a hand down his face in frustration. A fishing line zipped by his face again and he jerked to the left to avoid it. If only the old guys would watch what they were doing!

"There's no judgment, son, if you did. Just want you to remember that I'm always here for you and your brother."

Pete laughed suddenly and harshly. "You keep saying that. I've barely seen you since the divorce. You're not here for me or Chuck. You and Mom expect me to take your place with him." Pete thought he would feel better after getting the truth out, but he just felt bad. There was a funny feeling in his chest, like someone putting a hand there and pushing hard.

Dad's shoulders slumped. "That's not true, Pete. I live across town and you know I work odd hours. I'm doing the best I can. You and Chuck need to know that. I mean . . . I'll try harder. I love you both."

Yeah, Pete heard that a lot from both of his parents, but words weren't enough anymore. If Pete wanted to, he could really just cry right now. But crying hurt even worse than getting mad, so he decided on the mad.

"*This*," Pete lifted his bandaged arm to his dad's face, "was a freak accident. There were witnesses, okay? Unless I used my mind to make a buzz saw blade fly at me and try to take my hand off? *Right!* Not freaking possible. Just take me home, Dad. I'm done!"

"Please calm down, Pete."

"Please, just take me home." Pete stood so quickly that his folding chair skidded back. A gust of wind blew against him, almost taking his hat. He grabbed it before it could float away. Then he heard a very faint sound before something sharp tore into his cheek just below his eye.

Something tugged his face forward. "Ahhhhh!"

"Pete!"

He dropped his pole as his hands flew to his face to find a fishing hook stuck into his skin. The hook was attached to a fishing line, trying to pull his skin off. He leaned forward, screaming. Shock and pain flooded through him. His heart was pounding so fast he thought it might explode out of his chest.

The line was so tight, Pete stepped forward again to try and ease the pressure. There was only dark water below him, and he couldn't stop himself.

I'm going to go head first into the lake, he thought.

He felt his dad's arm wrap around him to keep him from falling. "Hold still!" His dad whipped out a small hunting knife and cut the line. The pressure instantly released.

Pete hunched over in severe pain. Blood dripped into the water.

His dad held him. "It's okay, buddy, I got you." He pulled him back away from the edge of the pier.

"I'm sorry!" someone called out. "Is he okay? The freaking wind blew my cast toward you guys. I can't believe it!"

"Pete, look at me. Come on, let's see the damage."

His dad leaned him back. Pete could barely see the hook sticking out of his face. His eyes watered, snot ran from his nose, and tears mixed with the blood dripping down his cheek.

Dad blew out a breath. "Oh yeah. Got you pretty good but you'll be just fine. We're lucky it didn't take out your eye."

So I guess Pete had a bad day.

Pete and Dad came home and Mom rushed to Pete. His face was all bandaged up.

Chuck's eyes widened. Wow, he almost looked like Frankenstein! But he'd have to save that nickname for another day.

"How did this happen?" Mom practically shrieked. "Oh, Pete, your poor face."

"Hey, there, Chuck, my boy!"

"Hi, Dad," said Chuck, and gave a little wave. He remembered when he was little and he used to climb his dad's legs till he picked him up. Chuck wondered when he stopped doing that.

Dad threw his hands in the air. "Now, Audrey, let's stay calm. It was a freak accident. A hook caught him in the cheek. It wasn't too bad, so I was able to patch him up myself."

Her eyes widened. "Another freak accident, on the same day? How is that even possible?"

Dad ran a hand down his beard. "Not sure. I think he needs to stay in bed, get some rest. I'm sure these accidents will pass."

"Yes, resting was what he was supposed to be doing," Mom snapped. "It was your bright idea to take him to the lake so he could get hooked like a fish. Why weren't you looking out for him?"

Dad whipped off his canvas hat, revealing his bald head. "Audrey, that's not fair. He was sitting *right* next to me. It was a windy day. A freak thing—"

Pete collapsed on the couch. He looked dazed as he watched Mom and Dad go back and forth, talking about him. Chuck wasn't used to seeing his brother look so . . . vulnerable. He was bigger than him, mouthy, and always annoying. Now, sitting on the couch, he seemed small and almost frail.

Chuck went and sat next to Pete, staring at his brother's face. "You look"—*like Frankenstein*—"bad, Pete. Does it hurt?"

"What do you think?" he muttered.

Chuck nodded as if he understood. "Pretty bad day, huh? So . . . what do you think is going on with you? Did you walk under a ladder? Break a mirror? Cross a black cat?"

Pete frowned. "What are you talking about?" he asked.

"What did you do to earn a streak of bad luck?"

Pete just shook his head. "It's not bad luck and I'm not accident-prone," he insisted. "I don't know what it is."

Chuck licked his dry lips and leaned closer to his brother. "It's something weird, though, right? First, you were sick, and Mom filled me in about the weird accident with the construction site, and now this fishing thing." Chuck had been thinking about the weird stuff that had piled up in his brother's life—it had all the makings of a really good puzzle. "This all started when you tried to scare me at Freddy Fazbear's Pizza," he pointed out.

Pete tried to scowl, but he winced as the gesture hurt his face. "What? Now you're trying to say this is something like karma? Bull. No way. I don't believe in that stuff."

Chuck shrugged. "You can't deny it's weird."

Pete was silent a moment, then said quietly, "It wasn't just those things."

Chuck raised his eyebrows, intrigued. "What do you mean?"

Pete shook his head. "Can't talk about it now. I'll tell you later." He nodded toward his parents as if he didn't want them to hear.

Chuck went to his room, sat on the floor in front of his TV, and started playing video games. He didn't really think Pete would tell him anything more, but a couple of hours later, Pete walked into his room and sat on his bed. His cheek was puffed out below his eye and his eyes were bloodshot.

Chuck paused his game and just looked at him, waiting.

"In school yesterday, I slipped and fell in biology class. I kicked a kid and his scalpel went flying. When I hit the ground, the scalpel was going for my eye."

Chuck's mouth dropped open. "No way."

"I knocked it away before it could hit me."

Chuck was impressed. "Quick thinking."

Pete looked pleased for a second. "Yeah, when you got the skills . . ."

"What else?"

Pete shrugged. "I went to pick up the chops at the butcher for Mom, and there wasn't anybody behind the counter. So I walked in the back trying to find someone. Out of nowhere, a cleaver falls from a hook and slams into the butcher's block by my hand."

"Holy cow! That's close!"

"Yeah, crazy close. I mean, if I believed in weird stuff, I'd think something was up. But I don't believe in anything like . . ."

"Curses?"

Pete frowned. "Get real, Chuck."

Chuck sighed. Why did he have such a stubborn brother? "What else can explain this? Four times? It's got to be *something*. Come on, Pete."

"Whatever it was, I'm done with it." Pete cleared his throat. "Just in case, it's because of, you know, dragging you to see Foxy." He stuck his hand toward Chuck.

Chuck's eyes widened as he looked at it.

Pete lifted his eyebrows. "Well? Shake."

Might as well, Chuck thought. Hesitantly, he took his brother's hand and shook it.

Pete took his hand back and even apologized. "I'm sorry about trying to scare you. It was dumb. Let's call a truce between us, okay?"

Chuck smiled. "Okay, truce. Thanks, Pete."

Pete stood up unsteadily. "I'm going back to bed. Later."

"Later," Chuck murmured, as his brother walked out of his room. Then he started thinking, rummaging through his desk for a notebook to write in. His brother may want to brush off all of his ideas but there had to be an explanation. There had to be.

"What game are you playing?" Pete asked Chuck from his bedroom doorway. He'd spent most of Saturday in bed and now he felt the need to get up and walk around the house. Lying in his bed gave him too much thinking time. He kept replaying each freak accident over in his head and it wasn't cool.

"Just an indie adventure game. Want to check it out?"

Pete shrugged and sat cross-legged with his brother on the floor. Chuck's room was a lot different than Pete's. First of all, Chuck actually used his hamper instead of dropping his clothes all over the floor. His bed was made. His desk was clear of extra paper. He had a bookshelf with books on aliens, and conspiracy theories. A couple of gamer posters were pinned neatly on the wall.

Chuck explained the game. "You see, I'm the mage, and I have to look for all the hidden ingredients to make a potion to stop an evil wizard. He has my village under a spell and I need to help break the curse with the potion and release the village before it's too late."

"What happens if you're too late?"

"Then I lose them forever. They remain under the control of the evil wizard. And that is *not* happening."

Pete smirked. "You like to be the hero, don't you?"

"It's the only way to win. Want to play with me?"

"Sure."

Chuck's eyes lit up as he grabbed the other controller. "You can be my apprentice."

"Why am I the apprentice? Why can't I be the mage and you be the sidekick?"

Chuck shook his head. "You have a lot to learn."

Pete turned to their mom, who was leaning in the doorway. She was smiling.

"Hey, Mom," Pete said.

"You guys need anything? How about some popcorn?"

"Could use some popcorn, thanks."

"And a juice box for me," Chuck said.

Pete played the game for a couple of hours and then went back to bed. He had to admit it was nice to get along with his little brother again. After shaking hands and calling a truce, it was almost like it used to be when they were little. When they didn't have a care in the world. Before the resentments, the name calling, the divorce. He had to admit he missed those days.

Before Pete knew it, Sunday night rolled around and he started getting ready to go back to school. To his relief, the swelling in his face had gone down. He'd removed the bandage from his arm, exposing a fresh scab on the wound right above his wrist. It made him think of his dad accusing him of hurting himself. Sure, thoughts of escaping his parents crossed his mind sometimes, but not the way his dad was thinking.

Pete had spent most of the day binge-watching TV. He hadn't dared to leave the house, afraid he'd have another freak accident. Not that his mom would have let him leave, anyway. She'd kept a close eye on him all weekend, really stepped up for him. Maybe he'd cut her some slack when she started piling on a bunch of stuff for him to do again.

If all these freak accidents had been some weird karma thing, he'd apologized to Chuck, hadn't he? So that meant he should be free and clear of whatever it was. But he still had a feeling that lingered in his gut like a sickness. He worried that everything might not be over.

That it might never be.

Then there was a knock on his door.

"Come in," he called out, and Chuck stuck his head in. Normally, he'd yell at him to get the heck out of his room, but things were different with the truce. Picking on his little brother didn't seem as much fun anymore. Not that he'd tell him that.

"Yeah?" Pete said.

His brother stepped in with a notebook in one hand and closed the door behind him. He fished his inhaler out of his shorts pocket, took a puff, then slipped it back in.

"How you doing?" he asked Pete.

"Okay, I guess."

"You ready to go back to school tomorrow?"

"Yeah, right."

Chuck flashed his braces and ran a hand through his hair. "Just checking."

"What's up with the notebook?"

"Something I've been working on this weekend since you told me about the accidents." Chuck walked over to Pete, flipped open his notebook, and showed him some sort of handwritten chart. There were five boxes arranged in a circle, with arrows pointing between them. On the top of the chart was a box labeled: FOXY THE PIRATE. The following boxes read: BIO CLASS, BUTCHER SHOP, CONSTRUCTION SITE, and LAKE. The final arrow pointed back to FOXY THE PIRATE.

"What's this mean?" Pete wanted to know.

"It means, I think the point of origin—where this all started—was in the maintenance room with Foxy."

"Yeah, we already talked about that."

"From there, each freak accident led to the next and now in order for this to be all over, you have to go back and fix whatever you did in the first place."

"I did. I apologized for the stupid prank, okay? Everything should be good now. You forgive me, right?"

"Yeah, we're brothers. Of course I forgive you," Chuck said. "But in all the games I play you have to face the ultimate bad guy. The villain. Just like with the game we played last night. The mage had to fight the evil wizard in the end in order to set the village free with the potion."

Pete forced a laugh as his stomach curdled in dread.

"Bad guy? Who? Foxy, the animatronic?"

"Maybe . . . but . . . what exactly happened after I ran out of there that day?"

Pete looked back at his TV, glimpsing an action movie. "Nothing, Foxy sang a song and then I left. No big deal."

You can be a pirate, but first you'll have to lose an eye and an arm! Yarg!

Pete's pulse picked up as he heard the words in his head.

"What was the song, Pete?"

He shook his head. "Just a stupid song about being a pirate."

"What were the words *exactly*?"

"Who cares what the words were?"

"I do. Please, Pete, it's important."

"*Fine.* Something about how if you want to be a pirate . . . you'll have to lose an eye and an arm. See? Stupid!"

Chuck licked his dry lips. Then he grabbed a pencil from Pete's cluttered desk and started writing.

"What are you doing?"

"Hold on a sec."

After a minute, he shoved the notebook into Pete's hands. Chuck had written additional notes under the boxes:

> FOXY THE PIRATE: Pirate song. Lose eye. Lose arm.
>
> BIO CLASS: Nearly lost eye.

BUTCHER SHOP: Nearly lost arm.
CONSTUCTION SITE: Nearly lost arm.
LAKE: Nearly lost eye.

Pete shook his head in denial. "No," he muttered as he started to shake. "You're wrong."

"You can't ignore the facts, Pete. Foxy wants you to become a pirate, and the accidents are getting more dangerous."

"No!" he yelled. "Foxy is a damn robot! He's made of metal and gears." He ripped out the page of the notebook and started to shred it. "This is all made up in your messed-up gamer brain. It's fantasy! Not real!"

"Pete, stop!"

"Shut up! Just get out of my room!" He shoved his brother and threw his notebook at him.

Chuck stumbled back in shock, his face turning red. "I'm trying to help you!"

Pete jammed a finger in the air toward Chuck. "No, you're trying to scare me for the all times I've scared you! It's always winning with you, right? Well, this isn't some game for you to win!"

"I know that. I'm not trying to win. I'm trying to figure this out!"

Mom appeared at the door. "Boys, what's all the yelling? What's going on?"

"Tell Chuck the Chump to get out of my room!"

"Don't call me that, Frankenstein Face!"

Pete's face scrunched up. "Oh, you've been waiting to use that one, haven't you? You're going to pay for that! Truce is officially over!"

"Fine by me! You can take your stupid truce and jam it up your nose!"

"Boys, calm down!" Mom yelled.

"I said, GET OUT OF MY ROOM!"

"I AM!" Chuck scooped up his notebook and ran out.

Pete turned his back to his mom. After a moment, with an exaggerated sigh, she closed the door.

Pete was so freaking angry, he started to cry.

Pete tossed and turned in bed, since his mind was wide awake. His pajamas felt too warm, his blankets too heavy. His bedroom was dark except for the moonlight that filtered through the curtain on his window. As he stared at the curtain, he thought he saw something dark flash behind the fabric.

Pete got to his feet and walked to the window, pushing the curtain aside. The front yard was quiet. A car was parked at the curb. A row of trees lined the street. Nothing out of the ordinary. He rolled his shoulders to release his tension, then went back to bed. He hit his pillow a couple of times to get comfortable. Then he stared at the ceiling and stared some more.

No use, he still couldn't fall asleep.

A moment passed as he found his eyes lured back to the window.

Don't get up. Don't look.

But he couldn't help himself—something felt strange. He was alone in his room, but he felt like he was being watched. Which was completely stupid. Sighing, he stood and walked back to the window, again pushing the curtain aside. He was about to step away when he caught a movement behind the trees. Was someone there?

Pete's pulse raced.

He rubbed his eyes, blinked, and searched for more movement—but nothing was there. His mind was messing with him. He was freaking paranoid! He took a breath and released it. It was probably just the wind blowing the branches. He scrubbed his hands down his face and lay back down in bed. The wind howled, and somehow that calmed him a little.

Then the backyard gate creaked.

The gate must have come unlatched in the wind . . . right? Just to be certain, Pete listened carefully. An owl hooted. A door creaked. A second later, he jerked upright, his heart pounding. Was that creaking inside the house? He crept to his bedroom door, and slowly opened it. He searched the empty hallway. No one was lurking around.

He was starting to really freak himself out. Mom and Chuck were asleep. No one else was in the house. *Just go to sleep!* he told himself. He stomped to his bed, threw himself down, and squeezed his eyes shut.

He thought he heard a footstep.

Just go to sleep.

The floor creaked outside his door and a chill crept down his spine.

No one else is here.

He told himself it was just his imagination, but the air seemed to shift around him. The hairs on his arms stood up and he couldn't deny his unease anymore.

When he opened his eyes, Foxy stood above him!

Terror sucked the air from Pete's lungs. He couldn't move. Couldn't speak.

Foxy's yellow eyes glowed in the darkness of the room. His jaw hung open, flashing sharp teeth. Foxy lifted his hook and slashed the sharp tip in front of Pete's face, the metal whizzing by his nose. Pete shoved himself off the bed, his body shaking, but he couldn't get off the floor. Foxy pivoted, looming over him. The shifting of gears filled the room as Foxy swung up with his hook.

You can be a pirate, but first you'll have to lose an eye and an arm.

"No," Pete breathed.

Foxy slammed his hook into Pete's eye, and there was an audible pop. Blood poured from his eye socket as Pete screamed. Foxy's mechanical foot slammed onto his right arm, crushing muscle and grinding against bone. Pete convulsed in agony. He tried to push Foxy off of him. Too heavy. Too strong.

Pete's heart pounded. Tears and blood ran down his face.

Foxy hacked down, his hook tearing into Pete's hand,

splintering bone and tearing muscle until it was ripped off completely. Foxy lifted his hook and watched Pete's hand dangle, blood spilling down.

Pete screamed.

He woke up screaming into his pillow. Since he was finding it hard to breathe, he bolted up, gasping for air. Sweat stuck his shirt to his skin. Sunlight was beaming through his window. He was home. In his bedroom. Alone. He spread his hands out—fingers wide—and saw that they were attached. He reached for his eyes, and both were still there. He was alive and he could see. All body parts were intact.

He took a deep breath of relief.

Just a nightmare.

Why did it have to seem so real?

Pete swallowed hard as his stomach turned and he started to tremble.

He felt as if he'd had a version of the same dream before, but this time he remembered every detail.

With a hood pulled over his head, Pete walked into North Hillside High School on Monday morning and gaped at the huge sign hanging in the hallway: FIND YOUR TREASURE ON THE HIGH SEAS—HOMECOMING CARNIVAL TODAY AT LUNCH. A pirate head was drawn under the slogan saying, "Aye, Matey!" while flashing a hook for a hand. Pete nearly turned around and walked home. But he knew how nervous his mom had been when she'd dropped him off at school.

"Everything is going to be okay, Pete," she'd said, like she was trying to convince herself.

"Yeah, Mom, everything will be fine," he'd reassured her. "Mom?"

"Yes, honey?"

"You're a good mom."

She blinked rapidly and smiled. "Thank you, son, you make me very happy."

The truth was, he hoped everything would be fine. He realized that all he wanted was to have everything back to normal—with boring classes and unnecessary tests and even taking care of his little brother. He was ready for it all to be over, and now he could see that he had an okay life even if his parents weren't together. His parents loved him and Chuck, even though they were often wrapped up in their own worries and obligations. He had a nice and comfortable home. A few friends. He wasn't one of those kids to make the best out of high school, but he'd get through it like everybody else. He walked farther down the hall, taking in the posters on the walls. There were pirate ships, parrots, skulls and crossbones, and pirate heads everywhere he turned. The student council always went all out for Homecoming week.

He could feel people gaping at the mess on his face, but he tried not to pay attention as they whispered and pointed. He walked to his locker and spun the combo, taking care to avoid a kid in a pirate's costume and an eyepatch. He unloaded some overdue homework from his pack, then pulled out his biology book for his first class.

"Dude, what happened to your face?" Duncan Thompson asked him. Duncan was Pete's locker neighbor, a short and stocky dude with a buzzed head—they used to play football together. For his version of school spirit, he had skulls and crossbones painted on both of his cheeks.

Pete shrugged as he shut his locker. "Fishing accident. No big deal."

"Like, how? You get cut with a knife or something?"

Pete didn't want to go into the details. "Something like that."

"Makes you look so gnarly, though. Like nobody should mess with you. You know what I mean?"

Pete cracked a smile. "Cool."

"Gonna miss you at the Homecoming game this week, dude. You would have looked pretty intimidating on the field, sporting a fresh scar on your face."

"Yeah, thanks," Pete said.

Duncan smiled and held up his fist. Pete bumped it.

He walked away from his locker feeling a little better. He held his head high as people watched him, ignoring the stupid pirate decorations and costumes. Yeah, he had the "don't mess with me" vibe going on and he liked it.

Pete's morning classes went smoothly. He didn't dare get up from his seat during class, and he stayed far away from any sharp objects. When the lunch bell rang, he felt surprisingly good, as if he really did end his streak of freak accidents. Now he just needed to make amends with his little brother . . .

The worst part was that he *had* made amends before he'd blown it again by yelling at Chuck and kicking him out of his room. He just didn't want to believe what Chuck believed—that it all wasn't over yet. That he had to go back to face Foxy.

Pete shivered. He'd apologize to Chuck and reinstate their truce. And Chuck would understand, he was pretty sure. His little brother seemed to forgive him easily. Pete was really ready to start fresh, as his mom would say sometimes. It would be like a new beginning. He never really understood what she meant by that until now.

The sun was out as he stepped out into the school courtyard where the carnival was happening. Food booths and games were set up and spread about. Kids roamed around eating cotton candy and junk food. There was a water dunk tank with their vice principal, Mr. Sanchez, waiting to be dunked. A pie-eating contest was set up, along with an arm-wrestling table, water-gun races, and more. A DJ was playing music and giving away T-shirts. Pete pulled off his hood and walked around hoping to find something good to eat. Not long after he started browsing, he ran into Maria.

She was working in a booth. "Oh, hi, Pete!" she said. She was wearing a red scarf around her head and big, round earrings. "Whoa, what happened to you?" She pointed to her own cheek.

"Hey, Maria." Pete shrugged. "It was a dumb fishing accident."

"Ouch, that sucks. Seems like you haven't been around that much."

Pete's eyebrows raised. She had noticed? "Uh, yeah, some stuff going on. Everything's cool, though."

She nodded as if she understood. "So, you want to win something? All you have to do is stick your hand in this box and see what you get." She nodded at a large table with a hole in the center.

Pete stuck his hands in his jean pockets. "No, it's cool. I'm good."

She smiled. "Come on, it's just for fun. Don't you want a prize?"

Pete's stomach quivered as he pulled out his right hand, closing his grip into a fist. All the freaky stuff was over, he assured himself. He was safe now.

"Sure, I guess." Hesitantly, he stuck his hand in the hole, and after a few seconds it was surrounded by something. "What the heck?"

Maria let out a small laugh. "What'd you get?"

He tugged his hand back but it was stuck. He pulled harder and the grip on his hand tightened. Unease rippled through him. Sweat sprouted on his forehead. Pete planted his feet and tugged so hard the table started to lift.

"Pete, stop! You're going to break the table!" Maria said.

"My hand's stuck!"

"I know, Pete, calm down." Maria knocked on the table really hard. "Okay, stop! I said to stop!"

Suddenly, Pete got his hand out and it was attached to something that looked like a Chinese finger trap, except it was big enough to cover his entire hand. Pete stared at it in disbelief. The stronger he had pulled, the tighter the trap had gripped his hand.

Maria looked guilty. "I'm sorry, Pete, it's just a joke we've been playing on the students. You know, just a little fun for Homecoming. Everyone else thought it was funny."

"I'm not everyone else," he snapped.

A kid popped his head out of the hole in the table. His hair was spiky and he had an earring in his nose "Dude, relax. Take a joke, why don't you?"

Pete didn't even know what to say, he was that freaked out. "Not cool!" he stammered, trying to pull the trap off his hand. Somehow it just gripped tighter, squeezing off his circulation. He swallowed hard. It felt like tiny knives poking under his skin. "Get this off of me!"

"Wait, I'll help you. I know how to do it." Maria rushed out of the booth to Pete and pushed the trap closer to his hand so that it would eventually loosen. "I'm sorry you're so upset."

"Yeah, right! Just get it off already," he said, barely holding it together.

"I'm trying, okay? It's stuck for some reason. Hold on." She ran back around the booth to grab something.

It wasn't just stuck, it was squeezing tighter and tighter. His hand started to throb with pain. *Not again*, was all he could think.

"Hey," the kid in the box whined. "Don't cut it. Then we can't use it anymore."

Maria came back with scissors. "I have to, it's not coming loose." She cut from the open end of the trap until she finally freed his hand.

By the time she got it off, Pete's skin looked completely purple and felt completely numb. He opened and closed his grip to get the circulation going again.

Maria's eyes widened. "Oh my gosh, Pete! I'm so sorry! I can't believe this happened. It's a freak—"

"Don't say it," he cut her off. "You just shouldn't have done that. You shouldn't have tried to trick me. I thought we were cool."

"We are . . ." When her cheeks reddened and she bowed her head, Pete's throat tightened. "I said sorry, Pete."

"Look, whatever. No big deal. I gotta go." Then, before she could say anything else, he stormed off, trying to calm his nerves as he rubbed his hand. What a stupid joke. How was that even funny? And it was another freak thing. He swallowed hard as his throat squeezed even more. He couldn't take any more accidents. He just couldn't or he'd lose his mind.

A rush of kids suddenly surrounded him like a herd of cattle, shoving him through the doorway of a mirror maze as they ran inside.

"Hey, watch out," he yelled. He tried to get out of the pack but there were too many of them. He just pressed against the wall as they finally passed by, laughing and screaming.

"Dude, look, there's like twenty of us in the mirrors!" someone called out as they disappeared.

Pete tried to get back out through the entrance, but somehow he found himself lost in the freaking mirror maze. He walked in the opposite direction to get directly to the exit. Instead, though, he came to a dead end, and a pirate appeared in the mirror, with a hat slanted to cover his face and a lethal hook attached to his arm. When he finally moved the hat, Pete could see that the pirate had the face of a fox. Pete flinched. He looked behind him, thinking the fox pirate would be standing there, but there was only another mirror.

His heartbeat picked up speed and his brain emptied of every thought but one: *Have to get out of here*. He turned and turned down narrow corridors, fleeing for the exit. Images of the fox pirate and himself were reflected in every mirror. When he ran, the fox ran. Sweat dripped down Pete's face. All he knew was that he couldn't let the fox pirate catch him.

He was breathing hard when he finally saw a light at the end of a small mirrored corridor. But before he could get there, the fox pirate jumped in front of him, raising his hook.

As if by instinct, Pete reared back and punched the fox pirate in the nose.

Then the pirate stumbled back, a hand to his mask, as Pete rushed out.

Pete was practically hyperventilating as he stepped back into the carnival. He was unsteady and off balance, as if he'd just come off a carousel. Kids laughed and stared as questions circled around and around in his mind. *Where do I go? What do I do?* He stepped backward and collided with someone. He whirled around to see a clown with a pirate hat. The clown waved, but Pete shoved him and ran toward a tent, pushing through the flaps of the heavy canvas. He needed to get out of the carnival but he was so mixed up he didn't know where he was going. He found himself rushing into a booth with several balloons pinned to a wall.

A dart came at him and scraped his cheek. He hit the next one away with his hand.

Someone yelled "Hey, there's a kid there!"

Pete himself sprang forward to tell them to stop, but it was too late. That was when the last dart hit home—sticking into the skin beside his inner eye.

He yelped in pain.

Kids gasped. Someone screamed.

Pete reached up slowly and pulled the dart out. A trickle of blood dribbled down his face. He threw the dart down and sprinted out the other end of the tent, panicking. He ran into another tent. Exotic birds were caged inside, tweeting and squawking.

A parrot shrieked: "Lose an eye! Lose an arm!"

Pete halted and whirled toward the bird. His body was shaking. "What did you say?"

"Squawk! Squawk!" The bird was bright green with a black beak. It flapped its wings at Pete. *"Squawk!"*

Pete grabbed the cage and shook it. Feathers scattered. All the birds in the tent started to go crazy. "What did you say, you, stupid bird? Foxy, are you in there?" No, it didn't make any sense for Foxy to be inside the bird, but Pete didn't care. Since when did any of this make sense at all? Whatever was happening to him was *still* happening to him and he'd had enough. "You're not going to win! You hear me? You. Are. Not. Going. To. Win."

"Hey, kid, take it easy!" Someone grabbed Pete's shoulder and turned him around. "What's the matter with you?"

Pete pulled away from the man, a teacher at the school. Mr. Berk or something like that. "Nothing's the matter." Pete wiped the sweat from his forehead and blood from his cheek. "Nothing."

Nothing except for a chain of freak accidents that involved losing an eye or an arm. Nothing except for a robotic fox that wanted him to become a pirate—or dead—whichever came first. Chuck had to be right. He had to get back to face Foxy to finish this once and for all.

Mr. Berk reached out a hand. "You don't look too good. You're bleeding from your eye. Let's go to the nurse to get you checked out."

Pete pulled away. "No! I'm fine!" he insisted.

"All right, take it easy. What happened to your cheek?"

"Too much has happened to me." Pete just shook his head. "Too much." How could he begin to explain?

"I just want to help," Mr. Berk said. "What's your name?"

"No, you can't help me. No one can. He's after me and he's never going to stop. I believe him now, I thought I could fix it all by apologizing." Pete laughed bitterly. "Yeah, funny, huh? Like 'sorry' ever fixes anything. But I had to try, right?"

"Who's after you, kid? What's his name? We can sit down with the principal. Get this all sorted out. You just have to calm down, take a deep breath."

"You don't understand! There's no sitting down or talking! He's a freaking robot!"

Mr. Berk's eyes widened. "A robot? Help me to understand. Let's just sit down a moment. You can talk to me, okay? Sometimes we think things are worse than they really are. But once we stop and look at the whole picture, it's not that bad at all. Believe me, kid. Happens all the time."

"No, it's bad. *Really bad*. But I know what I have to do now. It'll all be over soon. I have to go back to the point of origin, where it all began. I have to face the villain." Before the teacher could stop him, Pete slipped away.

He booked it down the school hallway, drenched in sweat. A hall monitor yelled for him but Pete ignored what he was saying. *Had to get out. Had to end this.* When he shoved open the doors, looking back over his shoulder, the hall monitor was talking into his radio. Pete missed a step and fell, stumbling down the school's front steps. His knees and palms were scraped, and his body felt bruised, but he pushed himself to his feet to keep running.

As he raced across the school's lawn, he dug out his phone and clicked on Chuck's number. It went straight to voice mail because Chuck was still in class.

"Chuck!" Pete heaved into the phone, short of breath. "You were right! It's been Foxy all along. I have to go back to face him! Freaky stuff is still happening, but no way is Foxy going to win, Chuck. No freaking way! I'm sorry I didn't believe you, little bro! Meet me there as soon as you can! We can finish this together!"

In a blind panic, Pete rushed off the sidewalk and into the street. He sensed something speeding toward him and he turned—that's when a truck smashed into him with extreme force. His body went flying, his limbs twisting, and one moment felt like forever. Then he crashed, his body slamming the hard ground. He felt a crack, then a shatter. The force scalded his skin against the road as he rolled and rolled, leaving a path of blood behind him. Pain was everywhere, then everything went dark.

"Chuck! You were right! It's been Foxy all along. I have to go back to face him! Freaky stuff is still happening, but no way is Foxy going to win, Chuck. No freaking way! I'm sorry I didn't believe you, little bro! Meet me there as soon as you can! We can finish this together!"

Chuck clicked off his phone, looked over his shoulder, and nimbly hopped his middle school's fence. Then he ran.

He had to get to Freddy Fazbear's Pizza. He had to help Pete!

He pumped his arms hard and fast to get out of sight of the school. When he felt safely out of view, he pulled out his inhaler, took two puffs, and walked till he caught his breath. He still had a few miles to go. He wished he had his bike, but he didn't, and he wouldn't let Pete down. He wouldn't let him face Foxy alone.

He started to run again, but that didn't last long. He wasn't much of an athlete. Chuck could run but it was usually short distances—he always did poorly in the timed mile in gym class. He glanced around, and stiffened up when he saw a police car. *Oh no!* He ducked into a donut shop and waited for the cruiser to drive by. He wasn't used to breaking the rules and ditching school. This was the first time he'd done something like this. What would happen if Mom found out? Would she ground him? Pete would probably laugh at him for being so scared. But that was okay, Pete could laugh at him all he wanted once this was all over.

He was out of breath when he got to Freddy Fazbear's Pizza, and his shirt was stuck to his back with sweat. He pushed through the front doors and felt relief when the cool conditioned air hit his face. Little kids were running around as he made his way to the corridor that led to the maintenance room. There was some sort of manager standing in front of the walkway. *Dang it.* Chuck bounced on his feet, waiting for the guy to walk away. He pretended to play an arcade game until the guy finally moved along.

Chuck walked slowly to the doorway, slipped through, and raced down the corridor until he got to the door. It swung open to reveal absolute darkness. Chuck swallowed hard as he stepped inside and the door slammed behind him. Fear nearly swallowed him whole, but he grabbed his phone from his pocket to turn on a light.

"*Hiccup.*"

He smacked a hand to his mouth to try and stop the dumb hiccups. He flashed the phone light to the left and to the right. No freaky ghosts, no robots. He took out his inhaler and took a quick puff as he continued to look around. Still the same dusty tables with old supply boxes and broken chairs, like the first time they had visited. For some reason, that felt like weeks ago.

"Pete," he whispered. "Where are you? *Hiccup.*"

When there was no answer, he wondered if Pete was trying to scare him again. Then he pushed that thought away. Pete had sounded really upset on the voice mail. He'd been physically hurt, and he finally believed Chuck's theory that it all began with Foxy. They were finally agreeing on something. Now Pete was treating him like a real brother instead of a problem he had to deal with every day.

"*Pete. Are you here?*"

When he was answered with silence, Chuck dialed his brother's number. It rang and rang, finally going to voice mail.

"Pete, where are you? *Hiccup.* I'm here with Foxy, waiting for you. Call me. Or just hurry up and get here. You know this place gives me the creeps. *Hiccup. Hiccup.*"

Chuck ended the call and stepped forward, aiming the phone light at the small stage. A chill ran through him and he shivered. Instinct told him to move far, far away from the stage. To get out. He couldn't, though. This wasn't about his fears. This was about his brother. Swallowing hard, he walked over to the control box. He would find out what happened to Pete that day. He really needed to know if Foxy was somehow haunting his brother. His hand was hovering over the START button when his phone rang and he jumped in the air. "*Hiccup—hiccup—hiccup.*" He quickly answered. "Pete?"

"No son, it's Dad. Where are you? I went to school to get you but you weren't there."

Chuck was suddenly scared he would get in trouble for ditching. His throat tightened. "Um, I'm sorry, Dad, *hiccup,* Pete needed me. I had to leave. *Hiccup.* I won't ever do it again. I promise."

"Pete? What do you mean? Did you talk to him?"

"Um, not exactly. He left me a message to meet him. But he's not here yet. I don't know where he is. He won't answer his phone. *Hiccup.*"

"Oh, son . . . ," his voice broke.

"What? What is it, Dad?" A wave of dread washed over him. "Why were you picking me up at school? *Hiccup*."

"Chuck . . . there's been an accident."

Dad picked up Chuck at Freddy Fazbear's Pizza and drove faster than normal to Pete's high school. He didn't ask any questions about why Chuck was supposed meet Pete there. He said Mom had gone straight to the school when she got the call that Pete had been hit by a truck.

"Let's keep the ditching school from your mom for the moment," Dad said. "She doesn't need any more on her plate right now."

Chuck felt the guilt like a punch in the gut. "Okay, Dad. You have to understand it was for Pete. I would never do it otherwise."

"I know, son. Don't worry too much about it. Brothers look out for each other."

Chuck nodded. As they drove closer to the high school, Chuck spotted flashing lights. Police cars were blocking the street, and barricades were holding kids far away from the sidewalk.

Chuck swallowed hard. "Pete's gonna be okay, right, Dad?"

Dad pulled to the side of the road, a block away from the emergency vehicles, and shut off the engine. "He's going to be fine." But his voice sounded funny, like his throat was tight. His eyes looked scared and uncertain as if he didn't believe his own words.

Chuck rushed out of the car with his dad. They headed toward the flashing lights.

A police officer held up his arms. "Sorry, can't let you through."

"That's my son. I need to see him. My wife is here."

"Name?"

"Dinglewood. My son's name is Pete Dinglewood. He's the one who was hit."

The policeman nodded and let them in. They passed more emergency workers than Chuck could count, and a truck that was pulled to the side, with a huge dent in the front of the bumper. Chuck gasped and hoped that dent didn't come from hitting Pete. There was a man sitting on the curb, talking to a police officer. He had his hat in his hands, and he was crying.

Chuck glanced toward the middle of the street, and froze when he saw Pete's shoe lying there. It was a plain white sneaker, making the blood splattered on it horribly noticeable. All he could think was that Pete needed his shoe. Little black numbers on plastic folded cards were scattered around the road, like for an investigation. Chuck swallowed hard and followed his dad until they finally spotted his Mom standing by a gurney. Her back was to them and her shoulders were shaking.

"There's Mom," Chuck said, even though he was pretty sure Dad had already seen her. Dad rushed to her side and put his arm around her.

Chuck held back, afraid to see Pete on that gurney. He

pulled out his inhaler and took a puff before he got any closer. Behind the barricades, there were some other high school students. Some faces were in shock, some kids were crying, and some kids were in pirate costumes. *Pete probably loved that.* The thought made Chuck's lips twitch, but he couldn't bring himself to smile.

"Chuck," Dad said, reaching out a hand. "Come here, son." He was crying. He'd never seen his dad cry before.

Chuck didn't want to move. Didn't want to walk to the gurney. If he could have, he would have gone in the opposite direction. But he forced a step forward and then another. He felt dazed and in slow motion, as if he was walking through heavy syrup. When he finally reached his dad and mom, he moved between them for support.

Pete was laying on the gurney. His eyes were closed, and he looked incredibly pale. The scratches from the fishing accident stood out like angry red lines on his face, and he had fresh scrapes etched into his forehead. Chuck waited for his eyes to open. Waited for him to move, blink, anything.

"He's gone, Chuck," Dad said through tears. His words made Mom cry even harder.

A man in a white uniform shirt walked over to them. "I'm sorry for your loss. We can meet you at the hospital when you are ready."

Dad said, "Yes, thank you."

The man was wearing blue gloves. He grabbed the large

zipper at Pete's chest and pulled it up, sealing Pete into a large canvas bag. Just like that, Pete was gone.

Pete felt frozen, like he couldn't move any part of his body. Strangely, he didn't feel cold or hot or any pain. He was surrounded by darkness. There were distant voices . . . sounds of movement . . .

Hello? Where am I? he wondered.

Weirdly, he couldn't move his lips.

What the heck?

It seemed like a long time passed. Finally, he heard something like a zipping sound, then a bright light appeared around him. There was a man above him wearing clear goggles, a blue cloth cap, and a face mask covering his nose and mouth. Was he a doctor?

Hey, dude, you got to help me. I feel weird.

Pete figured he must be at the hospital. He'd been hurt by the truck. He remembered. He was trying to get to the pizza place, but he'd forgotten the rule his mom had ingrained in him since he was little. To look both ways before crossing the freaking street. Well, now he'd be fixed with some surgery. Relief flooded over him. He'd get fixed up and then he and Chuck would face Foxy together and then it would all be over. Finally.

Another man appeared above Pete, looking down with sad eyes.

"Poor kid. So young," he said.

"Yeah, hate it when they're young like this."

"Really a shame. Gives me chills sometimes."

"Because of your own kids, right?"

"Yeah, I'll be sure to give them an extra hug when I see them."

"Me too."

The two men lifted up Pete's body and set him on a hard table.

Hey, guys, for some reason I can't move. What's the matter with me? Did you give me something to numb me? This is kind of freaking me out and I've had a really bad week, you know? So please tell me everything is okay.

A terrible thought dawned on Pete. *Oh no, did the truck hurt my legs? Will I be able to walk again? Is that why I can't feel them? Why won't you talk to me, guys? I need answers! I need help!*

One man put his gloved fingers above Pete's eyes. "Weird."

"What?"

"I can't close his eyelids. It's like they're frozen open."

"It's happened before."

"Yeah, but I don't like it. I want 'em closed."

The other man laughed. "Suck it up, buttercup. We have work to do." He picked up a handheld screen. "One good thing, says here the kid's an organ donor."

Wait. What?

"Yeah, parts of him are going to some lucky recipients. He's young, his organs are healthy. We got to work fast, though."

No! There's a mistake! I'm okay! I'm not ready to give up my organs. Mom! Dad! Where are you? Don't let them do this to me!

The men grabbed large scissors and started to cut his clothes away. A few minutes later music filled the room.

Wait a minute . . . is this another nightmare? Am I dreaming? Please let this be a bad dream. Let this not be real. Wake up, now, Pete! Wake the hell up!

"You got plans, tonight?"

"Yeah, taking the kids to Freddy Fazbear's Pizza. They love that place."

"My kids love that place, too. Those animatronic things kind of freak me out, but the kids love 'em. Whatever makes them happy."

Stop! I'm alive! You can't take my organs before I'm dead! Someone help me! Please!

The first man grabbed a scalpel and placed its point onto Pete's chest.

"Oh, hold up a minute," the other man said, reading again from the screen.

"What's up?"

Oh thank goodness. Tell him this is all a mistake. Tell him I'm still alive. Tell him not to cut me open!

"We have an urgent case, in need of the eyes and one hand. Says here the kid is an exact match. The hand doesn't have much damage. It'll work but we got to put everything on ice quickly. The transport will be here before we know it. Let's do that first."

Noooooooo!

The man with the scalpel looked down at Pete. "Good job, kid. You're going to help a lot of people." He retrieved small forceps with his other hand. The second man turned on a small buzz saw, the blade spinning into a circular blur.

"Let's get to work."

Pete began to hear Foxy's music play in his head . . .

You can be a pirate, but first you'll have to lose an eye and an arm! Yarg!

Pete watched in helpless horror as the first man leaned down to take his eyes.

Four weeks later . . .
Chuck rode his bike to Freddy Fazbear's Pizza. The clouds were heavy and dark, and there was a cold bite in the air. When he'd come home from school, no one was there. Even though Chuck knew the house was empty, he called out, "Hello? Pete?"

The refrigerator answered back with a low hum.

The house wasn't very big, but it seemed huge and empty to Chuck. He used to want to be old enough to stay home by himself. Now that he'd gotten his wish, he wished for company.

Mom had finally been able to go back to work after weeks of crying. Dad was also at work. Somehow the grief of losing Pete had reunited his parents, and Dad had moved back home after the funeral. One day, Chuck watched them both clean up Pete's room. They picked up the dirty clothes, threw away some garbage, made his bed, and closed the door. It hadn't been opened since.

Chuck hadn't met up with his friends in a while. He was supposed to be home doing his homework. But something had been driving him to go back . . .

Back to Freddy Fazbear's Pizza. Back to see Foxy.

He'd never told anyone what he and Pete had really thought about Pete's freak accidents. How they believed the trouble had started, or why they had planned to meet at Freddy Fazbear's Pizza to face Foxy once and for all.

For weeks, Chuck had felt this heaviness on his chest, like he was supposed to do something that he never got to do, like he had a puzzle that was incomplete.

He'd replayed Pete's last message over and over since the funeral.

"Chuck! You were right! It's been Foxy all along. I have to go back to face him! Freaky stuff is still happening, but no way is Foxy going to win, Chuck. No freaking way! I'm sorry I didn't believe you, little bro! Meet me there as soon as you can! We can finish this together!"

Pete's death nagged at Chuck day and night. Sometimes, when he was sitting in class, the bell would ring and he'd realize the period was over before he'd noticed it had started. He was falling behind in every subject. Teachers stared at him, but no one said much. They all knew he'd lost his brother. They all knew he'd changed. Chuck sat alone at lunch, writing in his notebook, filling it with notes, ideas, and scenarios on what could have happened to Pete and how they could have stopped it all before Pete had . . . gone.

Well, no more what ifs. Chuck was done wondering.

He locked his bike on the bike rack in front of Freddy Fazbear's Pizza. When he stepped through the doors, the familiar scent of pepperoni wafted over him. The pings and musical game sounds vibrated around him. He walked through the arcade and saw a group of kids huddled around a game. That used to be him. He'd always loved this place—until that fateful day, when Pete dragged him down the corridor to the maintenance room and everything had changed.

He walked through the play area and over to the birthday tables and watched a couple of families sitting right in front of the stage. Everyone looked so happy. The little kids were eating pizza, enthralled by the show of the animatronics. Some were singing with their mouths full. The kids clapped and cheered after the song finished.

Chuck walked toward the corridor that led to the maintenance room. He looked over his shoulder to see if anyone was watching, then he slipped through. He walked slowly down the darkened hallway, past the old posters, until he reached the door. He reached out for the handle and his hand shook. He took a breath, and pulled the heavy door open, stepping into darkness.

The door slammed at his back, the sound echoing in his ears.

He pulled out his inhaler as his breaths thinned, and took a puff. Then he shoved his inhaler into his pocket and pulled out his phone light. He went straight to the small stage and straight to the open control box. No more wasting time.

A shiver crawled down his back, but he ignored it. If he hesitated, he knew he wouldn't do it and he'd been replaying this moment over and over in his head. He had to do it. He had to find out what happened to Pete.

"This is for you Pete," he said into the dark room. "I'll face the villain and beat the game."

He braced himself and slammed down on the START button.

He waited for the curtain to pull back . . . for Foxy to begin to sing . . .

But nothing happened.

All Chuck heard was complete silence.

DANCE WITH ME

The stars looked like tiny pinpricks of light shining through a sheet of black velvet. Kasey lay on her back on a low stone wall, staring up at the sky, feeling wonder at being even a small part of such a beautiful universe. She remembered a nursery rhyme from when she was little, there had been a coloring sheet in kindergarten with the nursery rhyme's words and a picture of smiling stars. *Twinkle, twinkle little star,* she thought. *How I wonder . . . what I am.*

"Kasey!" Jack's voice startled her out of her trance. "Look over there!"

Kasey sat up and looked at the brightly lit kiddie restaurant across the street, Circus Baby's Pizza World. A woman and two young children were standing outside its red door. The woman was fumbling with her purse.

"Let's go," Jack whispered.

Kasey stood up and casually crossed the street with Jack,

ducking into the alley next to Circus Baby's, close enough that she could hear the little girl chattering to her mother.

"I think Circus Baby is pretty!" the little brown-haired girl said. She was wearing a T-shirt decorated with Circus Baby's Pizza World's creepy-looking mascots.

"She is pretty," the mother said, looking a little dazed, probably because she had spent too much time surrounded by the bright lights and loud noises of the kiddie pizza emporium.

"Can I wear pigtails like Circus Baby?" the little girl asked, pulling two handfuls of her hair up into bunches. She couldn't be much older than three, Kasey thought. Four, at the oldest.

"Sure you can," the mother said. "Hold your brother's hand while I find my car keys."

"Her hands are all sticky from candy," the boy complained. He was early elementary school age. Maybe seven.

"Mommy, I'm so sleepy," the little girl said. "Can you carry my goody bag?" She held up a little plastic bag with the name of the restaurant printed on it.

The mother had found her keys. "Sure," she said. "I'll just put it here in my purse."

"Can you carry me? I'm too sleepy to walk."

The mother smiled. "Okay, come here, big girl." Her purse dangled from her left forearm while she leaned over to pick up her daughter.

"Now!" Jack barked into Kasey's ear.

Kasey pulled the ski mask over her face and dashed out from her hiding place in the alley. She ran past the mother and grabbed her purse with a swift, sure motion. She kept running as the woman yelled "Hey!" and the little girl screamed.

As Kasey ran, she heard the little boy say, "I'll catch the bad guy, Mommy!"

"No," the mother said firmly. "You stay here."

If they said anything else, Kasey didn't stick around to hear it. Kasey knew she was fast, and she knew there was no way the mother could catch her on foot, not with two little kids on her hands.

After Kasey had put some distance between herself and the crime scene, she took off the ski mask and stuck it in her jacket pocket. She slowed to a walk and carried the purse casually, as if it belonged to her. And now, she supposed, it did.

She met the guys back at home, or at what passed for

home. Kasey and Jack and AJ stayed in an abandoned warehouse. There was no electricity—they had to make do with flashlights and camping lanterns. But there was a good roof, and the building was well insulated, which made it warmer than being outside. They slept in sleeping bags and heated food on a little two-burner cook stove, the kind people used on camping trips. Actually, living in the warehouse was a kind of indoor camping. That was one way to see it, Kasey thought.

She sat on one of the wooden crates they used as chairs, holding the stolen purse in her lap.

"How much did we get?" Jack asked, leaning over her shoulder. He was sharp-nosed and twitchy, like a rat.

"I like how you say 'we' even though it was me who took all the risks," Kasey said, unzipping the purse.

"That's the code of the Thieves' Den," AJ said, sitting on the crate next to her. He was big and bulky, the muscle of the group. "We share everything."

"Yeah," Jack said. "It's like how coaches say there's no 'I' in 'team.' Except it's there's no 'I' in 'thief.'"

"Yeah, but actually there is an 'I' in 'thief,'" Kasey said, laughing. She pushed her long braids out of her face and peeked inside the purse. The first thing she pulled out was the little girl's goody bag. No wonder the kid had screamed. She didn't want to lose all the candy and plastic junk she had "won" at the pizza place. Kasey stuffed the goody bag in her jacket pocket and then found what they were all waiting for: the woman's wallet.

"How much?" Jack said. He was trembling with anticipation.

"Hold your horses," Kasey said, unfolding the wallet and taking out all the bills. She counted. "It looks like . . . eighty-seven dollars." It wasn't great, but it wasn't terrible. People hardly ever carried cash anymore.

"What about cards?" AJ asked.

"I'm looking." She glanced briefly at the woman's driver's license, then looked away. She always felt bad when she thought of the victim as having a face and a name, of them having to wait in line at the DMV for a new license. She pulled out the plastic cards. "One gas credit card, one general credit card."

The gas card was of limited use since they didn't have a car. Still, they could use it in gas station food marts. And they could definitely get some use out of the credit card before they had to ditch it. Kasey badly needed some socks and a new pair of boots. The ones she was wearing were battered and held together with duct tape, so her feet hurt all the time.

"We'll try out the cards tomorrow," Jack said. "In the meantime, eighty-seven dollars split three ways is"—he made a big show of doing the math, "writing" in the air like he was solving a problem on the board at school—"Twenty-nine dollars each. I'll take twenty of that now, Miss Kasey. I'm gonna go out and see how much a person can party on twenty bucks. You two coming with me?"

"I will," AJ said. "Gimme a twenty, too, Kasey." He held out his hand.

"I think I'll stay here," Kasey said. She wasn't a partier like Jack and AJ. Her mother had partied a lot, and Kasey had grown up knowing that her mom's tendency to blow through all her money in one carefree night meant they had to have to live with the consequences until her next paycheck.

"Why?" Jack asked. "That's no fun."

"I'm tired." Kasey put the wallet back into the stolen purse. "I was the one who did all the running, remember?"

After the guys had gone out, Kasey lay on top of her sleeping bag and dug through the plastic sack from Circus Baby's Pizza World. She pulled out a pair of cardboard glasses with flimsy plastic lenses. The cardboard was decorated with a picture of some kind of weird robot ballerina. Kasey put the glasses on briefly, but they made her feel strangely dizzy. And if there was something she was supposed to be seeing, it was too dark to see it. She put them in her jacket pocket for later.

Everything else in the bag was candy. Kasey and her fellow thieves ate to survive. They had cheap fast-food burgers when they had a little money, canned beef stew or ravioli shoplifted from convenience stores when they were broke. It had been a long time since Kasey had eaten a piece of candy. She found a red lollipop, unwrapped it, and popped it into her mouth, enjoying the sweet artificial-cherry flavor and feeling like a little kid again.

A little kid. She had robbed a little kid. A saying came into Kasey's head: *like taking candy from a baby.* That's literally what she had done today. She wasn't proud of it, but at the same time, the kid's mom had nice shoes and a nice purse and a car. If she had enough money to take her kids out for pizza and arcade games, she could afford to buy her kids more candy.

Why had Kasey turned out the way she had, not like the woman she robbed? Kasey hadn't planned to be a thief who slept in a warehouse. She doubted those were anybody's career goals.

Kasey's mom hadn't been crazy about being a mom. She worked nights and slept days and often, when Kasey came home from school, her mom looked at her with a mixture of surprise and annoyance, as if she were thinking, *Oh, I forgot. I have a kid, don't I?* Dinner was usually a bowl of cereal or a sandwich before her mom went out to work at the club. While her mom was gone, Kasey did her homework, took a shower, and watched TV until bedtime. She had instructions to go to the apartment of the old lady next door if there was ever an emergency, but there never was. Kasey was good at taking care of herself.

When Kasey was a teenager, her mom got a new boyfriend who seemed like he was going to stick around longer than her past string of boyfriends. He had a steady job and could help her mom out with money. The only drawback was he didn't want a teenager around "freeloading," as he called it. He said he had moved out of his parents' house and gotten a job by the time he was Kasey's age, and that was why he was so successful. When he asked her mom to choose between him and Kasey, she didn't think twice about the choice. Kasey was out on the street before her seventeenth birthday.

Kasey's teachers had begged her to not to drop out of high school. Her grades were solid, and she was an athlete, so there was the possibility of college scholarships, they said. But she couldn't stay in school and still earn enough money to survive. She dropped out and drifted from one dead-end job to another, working long hours but never making enough to cover rent and groceries. Sometimes she stayed in sad little rooms she rented by the week; other times she camped out on friends' couches until their hospitality ran out.

The first time she stole was at Famous Fried Chicken, the fast-food restaurant where she was working. It was a terrible job. She stood sweating over the deep fryer for hours, and every night she went home feeling like she'd been dipped in a vat of grease. One day, when she was sweeping the floor of the dining area, she noticed that some guy had gone to the restroom and left his jacket hanging on the back of his seat. The corner of a twenty-dollar bill was peeking out of the pocket. It was too tempting.

Sweeping the floor right next to the table, Kasey pinched the bill and hid it in her sleeve. It was shockingly easy and somehow exhilarating. She knew the guy would never suspect theft. He'd just think that he should be more careful.

Making minimum wage, standing over the hot fryers, it would have taken Kasey more than two hours to earn the money that it took her less than a minute to steal. There was a thrill in that—to know you had gotten away with something, beaten the system.

Soon she was stealing instead of working—snatching purses, picking pockets, shoplifting food and other necessities. One day she was at a street festival, lifting wallets and loose bills from people's pockets, when two men approached her. At first she was scared they might be cops, but they didn't look like cops. One was a scrawny, fidgety white guy with lots of tattoos; the other was a broad-shouldered black guy with the appearance of a former high school football player.

"We've been watching you, and you're good," the thin, nervous-seeming one said. "Have you ever thought about working with a team instead of flying solo?"

"We look out for each other," the big guy said. "And we split our take. More people working, more money."

She fell in with Jack and AJ because they had been on the streets longer than she had and were willing to share their knowledge of how to survive. Sure, they were more reckless than she was, and blew through the money they stole, but there was safety in numbers. Even though the guys got on her nerves sometimes, she would rather have their companionship than try to make it on her own.

Kasey finished the red lollipop and snuggled into her sleeping bag. She fell asleep with the sweet taste still on her tongue.

She awoke to sunlight streaming through the warehouse's skylights. Jack and AJ were both still snoozing away in their sleeping bags. Kasey had no idea what time they had come in last night. She slithered out of her sleeping bag and decided she'd use two dollars from yesterday's take to buy a cheap breakfast at the Burger Barn. A sausage biscuit and a small coffee with free refills could last her all day if it had to. Kasey grabbed her backpack and walked into the bright morning sun.

The Burger Barn was just half a block from Circus Baby's Pizza World, the site of yesterday's heist. Kasey chuckled, thinking of it as something as dramatic as a heist, since it involved stealing a bag of candy from a child. She went inside the Burger Barn, placed her order, then sat down at an orange vinyl booth beneath a mural of cartoonish barnyard animals. She added cream and sugar to her coffee, unwrapped her biscuit, and took her time with breakfast.

As she nibbled her biscuit and sipped her coffee, she watched the other customers. Most of them were grabbing orders to go as they rushed off to their jobs at offices or stores or construction sites. They all looked stressed-out and in a hurry.

That was one good thing about Kasey's life. She could

take her time. The only time she had to hurry was when she was running off with somebody's purse or wallet.

Buying breakfast at the Burger Barn gave her the right to use the ladies' room without being kicked out. This was a right she treasured. After she finished her meal, she made her way to the restroom to do her grooming for the day. She locked herself in a stall and took a sort of sponge bath with baby wipes, then changed her socks, underwear, and shirt. After she was done in the stall, she went to the sink and washed her face and brushed her teeth.

A woman dressed in the button-down shirt and khakis of an office job gave Kasey a dirty look, but Kasey ignored her. She had as much right to be there as anyone else. Kasey filled her water bottle and put it in her backpack. She was ready for her day.

Out in the sunshine, her belly full of food and coffee, Kasey felt good. She thought she might take a walk in the park before she went back to the warehouse to see what the boys were up to. As she walked, she shoved her hands in her jacket pockets and felt the cardboard glasses from the little girl's goody bag. She smiled to herself and took them out.

She hadn't noticed that a tiny slip of rolled-up paper was taped to the glasses' left earpiece. She peeled the tape off carefully, unrolled the slip of paper, and read:

Put on the glasses, and Ballora will dance for you.

Kasey put on the glasses and felt the same dizziness as the night before. She looked down the sidewalk toward

Circus Baby's Pizza World. There, in the distance, she saw the image of a ballerina, her hands above her head, standing on tiptoe and spinning. It wasn't a very sharp image, blue and a little fuzzy. A hologram. That was what these kinds of pictures were called, she suddenly remembered. But even if distant and blurry, there was something fascinating about the strange ballerina doll twirling.

A pirouette. That was the word for that kind of twirling. When she was little, Kasey had wanted to be a ballerina, just like lots of other girls. But there had been no money, and her mother had said that even if there had been money, she wouldn't waste it on something as useless as dance classes.

Kasey stood on the sidewalk and watched the image as though hypnotized. It was beautiful, and there was so little beauty in Kasey's day-to-day life. Kasey felt overcome with sadness and longing and another feeling, too . . . regret? Was she regretting the way she lived? A life should have beauty in it, shouldn't it? Life should be about more than just survival.

After a while, Kasey started to feel dizzy, as if she were the one doing the pirouetting herself. Afraid she might be sick, she took off the glasses and leaned against the side of a building to get her bearings.

She looked down at the pair of glasses in her hand. Really, the ballerina was a pretty impressive visual effect for what looked like such a cheap toy. No wonder the little girl was upset when Kasey snatched her goody bag. To a little kid, these glasses would seem downright magical.

Kasey put the glasses in her pocket. She decided to skip the park and go back to the warehouse. She had to show the guys this crazy toy.

Jack and AJ were just waking up when she got back.

"What time did you guys get in last night?" Kasey asked, sitting down on a crate.

"Dunno. Two? Three?" Jack yawned. He propped up on one elbow in his sleeping bag. "It doesn't matter. I don't have to punch anybody's time card."

AJ unzipped his sleeping bag and sat up cross-legged on the floor. "Hey, we were just saying we might take that gas card you pinched up to the Gas 'n Go and see if we can use it to get some groceries."

"Sure," Kasey said. It would be good to have some food in the house. "But first I want to show you something."

Outside the warehouse, beside a dumpster, Kasey took out the glasses. "These were in the goody bag from the pizza place. Try them on." She held the glasses out to Jack.

Jack put them on, struck a "cool" pose, then laughed.

"Look in front of you," Kasey said. "Do you see her?"

"See who?" Jack said.

"The dancing ballerina."

"I don't see anybody," Jack said. "They just make everything look blue, that's all."

"Let me see 'em," AJ said, taking the glasses from Jack

and putting them on. He looked around. "I don't see anything, either."

"No ballerina?" Kasey said. It didn't make sense. Why could they not see her?

"Nope. Everything just looks blue, like Jack said." AJ handed the glasses back to Kasey.

Kasey was confused. Maybe the glasses only worked in front of Circus Baby's Pizza World? But that didn't make sense, either. Why would someone make a toy that only worked in one place?

She put on the glasses and looked straight in front of her, across the street. The ballerina—Ballora, according to the instructions—was there, dancing in a garbage-strewn alley between two warehouses. But soon the dizziness overcame her, and again there was that uneasy feeling she'd had before. "Well, I see her," Kasey said, taking off the glasses before she lost her balance or threw up. "Maybe there's something wrong with your eyes."

"Maybe there's something wrong with your brain," Jack said, laughing and elbowing AJ, who laughed, too.

Kasey ignored his ribbing and put the glasses back in her jacket pocket. But she did wonder. Were they right? Was there something wrong with her?

At the Gas 'n Go, they grabbed way more food than most people would buy in a convenience store: a jumbo loaf of bread, a jar of peanut butter, six bags of chips, cans of ravioli and beef stew, and a twelve-pack of soda. Kasey knew she would be the one to pay at the register because

Jack and AJ always said she had an honest face. Also, people were less likely to suspect a woman of criminal activity.

The cashier looked sleepy-eyed and bored as she rang up and bagged all the items. Kasey scanned the stolen card in the machine and held her breath. It took only a few seconds, but it felt like ages until the word "Approved" appeared on the screen.

Kasey, Jack, and AJ grabbed the bags and waited until they were outside the store to laugh at their good fortune. "Well, we won't have to worry about food for a few days," Jack said. "Hang on to that card, Kasey."

Kasey put the card in a small compartment in her backpack. "I will, but I don't know if we'll be able to get by with using it again," she said. Usually credit card companies were pretty quick to cancel cards they suspected were stolen.

Back at the warehouse, they feasted on peanut butter sandwiches and potato chips and soda that was still cold from the convenience store's cooler. Jack and AJ were still high from the adrenaline rush of successfully using the stolen card. They laughed and joked around, but something was bothering Kasey that she couldn't put her finger on. She smiled at Jack and AJ's jokes, but something that felt like worry was nagging at the back of her brain. The weird thing was that while she felt it, she didn't really know what she was worried about.

There was always the thief's worry of getting caught. The worry of being arrested, tried, jailed. That worry never went away, but this feeling was something else. Somehow it had to do with the glasses, with the fact that she could see the dancing ballerina while Jack and AJ couldn't, with the strange way looking at the twirling ballerina made her feel.

After they were finished eating, Kasey grabbed one of the plastic bags from the convenience store. "Put your trash in here," she said to Jack and AJ, "and I'll take it out to the dumpster."

"Always cleaning up after everybody. Such the little housewife," Jack said, dropping his empty soda bottle in the bag.

"Hey, I can't help it if you guys are slobs," Kasey said. "I don't want to get a bug problem in here."

Kasey had grown up in a series of progressively dumpier apartments. Her mom would get evicted for not paying the rent, and then they'd move to another place that was smaller and dirtier than the one before it. There were always cockroaches, and in the summer, an endless parade of ants. When Kasey got old enough, she washed the dishes and took out the garbage that her mom let pile up. Cleaning helped some, but bugs would still come over from other people's apartments like party crashers looking for free food and drink. Kasey always thought that when she grew up, she would have a neat little apartment of her own that would be clean and bug-free. Unlike her mom, she would pay the rent on time every month.

The warehouse wasn't exactly what she'd had in mind,

but at least she could do her part to keep the bugs away. She took the trash bag outside and tossed it into the dumpster.

Maybe she would take a walk. She felt a sudden need to be alone. She knew that, inside the warehouse, Jack and AJ would be making plans for the night. Since it was Friday, they'd probably want to go downtown to where the clubs were. If you waited late enough until people had been partying for hours, it was easy pickings. Kasey could walk past a cluster of guys and lift three of their wallets without any of them noticing.

Purses were always trickier because you couldn't grab them without the owner noticing. But Kasey was fast. She had been in track and field before she dropped out of high school. There was no way a tipsy girl in heels could catch her.

Usually Kasey liked to plan out the evening's job with the guys. She liked to strategize how to come up with the biggest take possible, how to maximize their chances of success. It was like solving a puzzle.

But right now she didn't feel like putting puzzle pieces together. She felt like walking, like clearing her head of the confusing thoughts swirling around inside of it.

Swirling. Swirling rhymed with twirling. Why couldn't she get that spinning ballerina doll out of her head?

She walked to the park. Office workers on their lunch breaks sat on benches and ate sandwiches. A dog walker was somehow walking four dogs of different sizes without getting their leashes tangled. Kasey smiled at the tiny Yorkie that was leading the pack as if it were the biggest dog of all.

On the playground, little kids climbed and slid and swung, shouting and laughing. Their moms watched them, making sure they were safe. Kasey envied those kids. What must it be like, she wondered, to play to your heart's content and to know that whenever you got hungry or thirsty, your mom would just pull some crackers and a cold juice box out of her bag? To know that, when you were tired, you could go home, and your mom would tuck you into your nice, soft bed for a nap?

Even as a little kid, Kasey had never known that kind of security.

She walked into the more wooded area of the park because she liked the shade and the solitude. The fall leaves—red, gold, and orange—were drifting down from the branches of the trees. Leaves that had already fallen crunched under her feet.

It was the strangest thing. She didn't want to see Ballora. She didn't like the way seeing Ballora made her feel. Yet she felt herself reaching for the cardboard glasses, felt herself putting them on. She felt the familiar dizziness, steadied herself against a tree, and stared into the woods in front of her, where sunlight sparkled through the gaps in the branches.

There was Ballora, pirouetting among the colorful fall leaves. As she spun, the bright leaves were sucked into her vortex. They flew around her, at first gently, then faster, as though trapped in a whirlwind.

For a few seconds, Kasey admired the beauty, but then she thought, *Wait. If Ballora is just a picture, a hologram, then how is she affecting the objects around her?* It didn't make sense.

Also, wasn't Ballora closer to Kasey than she was yesterday? It seemed like she was. The image was clearer, for one thing. Not so fuzzy—she could see the joints in the doll-like figure's arms and legs, could see the blue eyes and red lips on the white face. The painted face looked clown-like, but unlike most clowns, Ballora wasn't smiling. The empty blue eyes didn't blink, but somehow Kasey felt they were staring back at her. Ballora was looking at Kasey and didn't like what she saw.

Suddenly Kasey couldn't catch her breath. She doubled over, afraid she might pass out. Why was she freaking out over a stupid toy? She yanked off the glasses and shoved them back into her jacket pocket. She was being ridiculous, and she had to stop it. If you wanted to survive, you had to keep a cool head at all times.

She should go back to the warehouse and talk to the guys. She needed to know about the plans for tonight.

After midnight, Kasey, Jack, and AJ hit the clubs. They didn't go into them, but skulked in the darkness outside. The guys had targeted a couple of different bars, and Kasey was waiting in the alley outside a dance club that was frequented by a lot of college kids, their pockets and purses fat with their mommy and daddy's money.

She spotted her target. The girl was wearing a short, light-pink dress with impossibly high pink heels. Her designer purse—the same shade of pink as the dress and shoes—hung from a skinny strap draped over her shoulder. Pink Dress Girl was talking loudly and giggling with her boyfriend.

Kasey had a tool for jobs like these, a pair of strong scissors that could cut through a leather purse strap like it was only made of paper. She took out the scissors and stepped into the crowd. She slipped in behind Pink Dress Girl and positioned the scissors to cut the strap. As she snipped, someone bumped into her from behind. She slipped, and the point of the sharp scissors found flesh. When Kasey grabbed the purse, she saw a shallow but bloody gash on the girl's arm.

"Ow! What happened?" the girl yelled. "Hey, my purse—"

Kasey ran.

She ran until she was sure she had put enough distance between her and her victim, then slowed to a casual walk, tucking the pink evening bag inside her jacket.

In her mind, Kasey kept seeing the girl's arm slashed by the scissors, the red blood vivid against the girl's pale skin.

Kasey hadn't meant to hurt her. Sure, getting your purse snatched might scare you a little—might inconvenience you—but it didn't cause any physical harm.

Kasey had robbed dozens, maybe even hundreds, of people, but she had never harmed anyone physically until tonight. Spilling blood changed things.

It was an accident, Kasey thought. But was it really? The girl wouldn't have gotten cut if Kasey hadn't been lunging at her with the scissors. Kasey hadn't meant to cut her, but she couldn't exactly claim to be innocent.

Kasey beat the other guys back to the warehouse. She grabbed a flashlight and sat down on her sleeping bag to see what she'd scored. She opened the pink purse and dumped out its contents: a driver's license, a lipstick, and a single twenty-dollar bill which, according to Thieves' Den rules, would have to be split three ways.

Kasey put the items back into the purse and sighed. It hadn't been worth the effort or the bloodshed. She settled down in her sleeping bag, but it was a long time until she fell asleep.

The next day, Kasey and Jack and AJ walked downtown, casing possible places for a job. They walked past the park where Kasey had seen Ballora. Kasey glanced into a grove of trees and saw the leaves rise and swirl just like they had around the dancing doll. She put on her glasses, and there Ballora was, closer than before. She was getting closer every day. If Kasey could just get the guys to see the doll, she would feel a lot better. Kasey took off the glasses and hurried to catch up to Jack and AJ.

"Wait, you guys," Kasey said. She held out the glasses.

"Put these on and look over there, right in the middle of those trees."

"Again?" AJ said. "Not me. I love you like a sister, Kasey, but I'm done with this weirdness."

Jack rolled his eyes but said, "All right. Give 'em here." He put them on and looked where Kasey was pointing. "Nothing."

"Nothing?" Kasey's heart sank.

"Zilch. Zip. Nada," Jack said. "The way I see it, there are two solutions to this problem. One is locking you up in a soft room, and other is . . . this." He dropped the glasses in a nearby trash can. "There. Problem solved. Okay?"

Kasey felt a wave of relief wash over her. Jack was right. No glasses, no problem. "Okay." She even felt herself smiling a little. "Thanks, Jack."

"You're welcome," Jack said. "Now you need to pull it together. The Thieves' Den needs your quick wits and nimble fingers. No more freaking out over weird stuff."

Kasey nodded. She couldn't believe she'd let herself fall apart because of a cheap toy. "Quick wits and nimble fingers. You've got 'em," Kasey said, waggling her fingers. "Why don't we take the bus to the All-Mart and see if we can get that lady's credit card to work?"

"Excellent idea," Jack said. "See? You're better already."

The guys headed on toward the bus stop, but Kasey hesitated. The glasses were what made her see Ballora. Being rid of them, she wouldn't see Ballora. But that didn't mean Ballora wouldn't be there. She could still be following

Kasey—getting closer to her every day—but Kasey would have no way of knowing where she was. The thought of an invisible Ballora was scarier than the thought of a visible one. Kasey reached into the trash can, retrieved the glasses, and put them back in her pocket before she ran to the bus stop.

At the big box store, Kasey picked out a new pair of boots—heavy, comfortable, and practical. They all grabbed packages of socks and underwear and T-shirts. Buying too much stuff would arouse suspicion, so they tried to limit themselves to the things they needed the most.

As always, Kasey was the one to make the purchase because of her honest face. Her face didn't matter much, though, because the cashier rang up the items without looking at her, then asked robotically, "Debit, credit, or cash?"

"Credit," Kasey said, holding out the stolen card.

The woman scanned the card in the machine, frowned, then tried it again. "I'm sorry, ma'am. This card has been declined. Do you have another card you'd like to use today?"

"No thank you." Kasey grabbed the useless card, abandoned her attempted purchases, and walked quickly to the front door where Jack and AJ were waiting. "Declined," she said.

"Well, that sucks," Jack said as they walked out the door.

AJ shook his head. "The lady must've reported it stolen.

Too bad. I was kind of looking forward to my new socks and undies."

"Only one thing to do," Kasey said. She took out her big scissors, cut the card into tiny pieces, and scattered the confetti into the nearest trash can.

On the way back to the warehouse, they passed the park. Kasey heard the rustling of leaves and glanced over to see them swirling, but that didn't mean Ballora was there, she told herself. She clenched her hands into fists to stop herself from getting the glasses out of her pocket. The swirling leaves meant only that it was a windy fall day. That was all.

Tonight's job had to make up for their run of bad luck. They sat huddled in the warehouse, eating canned ravioli with their hands and trying to figure out their next move.

"We could try the pizza place again," Jack said. "People do take cash to those places."

"No." Kasey's response was automatic and forceful.

"Why not?" Jack said. "Afraid you might end up with some scary possessed toy?"

"It's not that," Kasey said. She probably deserved the mockery. She had let the thing with the glasses get out of control. "I just don't like to get kids involved, okay?"

"We've not done the train station in a while," AJ said. "It's real easy to mix in with the crowd there and pick some pockets. It might be a good way to get your confidence back, Kasey."

"Yeah, let's do that," Kasey said. That was what she needed. An easy job.

They didn't even have to go inside the station, just wait until rush hour when a bunch of people came spilling out of the station's exit, then slip into the crowd unseen. Kasey eased her way into the mass of people, scoping for prosperous-looking businessmen with wallet-shaped bulges in their back pockets. She had just found one and was reaching for it when someone grabbed her arm. She startled, then saw it was Jack. He mouthed the words *Let's go.*

When she saw the flashing blue lights, she understood.

A police car had pulled up to the curb. Kasey and AJ and Jack walked with the crowd, nice and casual, like they had just gotten off the train themselves. Kasey didn't breathe easy until the blue light was way behind them.

"Could this day have been any worse?" Jack said once they were back in the warehouse.

"Bad luck always comes in threes," AJ said, holding up three fingers. "So we've got two down and one to go."

"I don't believe in superstition," Jack said. "Not black cats, not broken mirrors. None of it."

It was chilly in the warehouse, warmer than outside, but still not warm. Kasey decided to keep her jacket on. It was getting nippier at night, and her hands were cold. Soon she'd have to buy or steal some gloves. She shoved her hands in her jacket pockets for warmth. There were the glasses. Where was Ballora? Was Ballora about to catch her? Was that the third piece of bad luck? Her heart pounded in panic, and she ran past Jack and AJ, out of the warehouse. Now the cold was the least of her worries.

Outside, she put her head in her hands and paced back and forth. Finally, with a shaking hand, she reached into her pocket and took out the glasses.

Because she couldn't help herself, she put them on. There, under a beam from a streetlight only a few yards away, Ballora twirled. She was closer than she'd ever been before. Kasey could see every joint in her body, each detail of her face, torso, and tutu. She was beautiful and horrible at the same time, and she was definitely getting closer.

Kasey tore the glasses off and shoved them back into her pocket. She sat on the cold, damp curb and tried to think. Each time she had seen Ballora, she had been a little closer. What was going to happen when Ballora got close enough to touch her? Could Ballora catch her?

Kasey felt like she was waiting for a punishment. She didn't know if it would be swift and sure or long and torturous. She didn't want to know.

There had to be a way to escape, Kasey thought. Ballora had appeared the first time outside Circus Baby's Pizza World, the scene where Kasey had stolen the glasses. Since then Ballora had stalked her throughout the city. Maybe, Kasey thought, Ballora could only follow her in the city where the crime had occurred. Maybe if Kasey could leave, go somewhere else, she could leave Ballora behind.

It was worth a shot.

Kasey waited until Jack and AJ were asleep, then sneaked into the warehouse and quietly rolled up her sleeping bag, grabbing her backpack of belongings. She took her portion of the money from the Thieves' Den hiding place and left Jack and AJ the rest. She wouldn't steal from them. They had been like brothers to her—annoying sometimes, but good to her in their own way.

It was a long walk to the bus station. She looked at the list of departures. The next bus leaving was headed for Memphis at 6 a.m. She guessed she was going to Memphis. She bought a ticket, which cost half of all her money, then settled on a bench to try to sleep a couple of hours. She woke at 4:30, aware of someone near her. She clutched her backpack to protect her belongings from people like herself.

"I'm sorry. I didn't mean to wake you up." The voice belonged to an elderly lady with gray hair and skin a couple of shades darker than Kasey's. She had on a butter-yellow flowered dress and a matching hat. She looked like she was going to church.

"It's okay," Kasey said. "I needed to wake up anyway. My bus leaves in an hour and a half."

"Where you headed?" The lady settled herself down next to Kasey.

For a second Kasey wondered if she should tell her, but the old woman's tone was so kind she didn't see the harm in it. "Memphis," she said.

"Oh, that won't be too long a trip," the lady said. "I'm going to Chicago to see my son and daughter-in-law and my grandbabies. It'll be a nice visit once I get there, but it's going to be one long bus ride. You got family in Memphis?"

"No, ma'am," Kasey said. "I'm just looking for a fresh start." It wasn't like she could tell the old lady she was running from a ballerina doll that possibly meant her harm. That would make the old lady move off the bench real fast.

"You got a job lined up?" the old lady asked.

"No, but I'll find something," Kasey said. "I always do."

"Good for you," the lady said, patting Kasey's arm. "I like to see a young person with some gumption." She picked up a big straw tote bag and started rummaging through it. "You hungry, baby? I packed enough breakfast, lunch, and dinner for an army. There's no way I'm paying for bus station food. It's expensive, it tastes bad, and it's bad for you."

Kasey was hungry. She hadn't realized it until the lady mentioned food. "I am a little, yeah. But you don't have to share if you don't—"

"I've got plenty, baby." From the bag she produced a small bottle of orange juice, cold and wet with condensation. Then she handed Kasey something wrapped in aluminum foil. "Ham biscuit," she said. "You're not one of those young people who won't eat pork, are you?"

"No, ma'am," Kasey said. "I'll eat anything that's put in front of me. Thank you." The biscuit was homemade and fluffy, and the ham was just the right amount of sweet and savory. It was the best food Kasey had eaten in a long time. "Delicious," she said.

"I'm glad you like it." The old woman patted Kasey's arm one more time, and then rose stiffly from the bench. "I'd better go to the ladies' room before I get on the bus. Those bathrooms on the bus are no fun. I like a bathroom that stays put."

Kasey laughed. "Yes, ma'am." It was the nicest conversation she could remember having in a long time.

The old lady looked at Kasey for a long moment. "Listen, I know it's not my place, but since I'm never going to see you again, I might as well say my piece. You seem like a young lady who's running away from something. In my experience, sometimes if you try to run away from your problems, those problems just end up following you. Does that make sense?"

Kasey nodded. She couldn't look into the lady's eyes.

"It's better to build bridges than to burn 'em, honey. You remember that."

The old lady tottered away, and Kasey felt a chill at the prospect of her problems following her. Of Ballora following her. She hoped with all her heart that the old lady was wrong.

Kasey slept through most of the long bus ride, waking occasionally to look out the window at the passing landscape. This was the longest trip she had ever taken, so she might as well enjoy the scenery.

The farther she traveled, the more hopeful she felt. A

fresh start. That's what she told the old lady she was headed for, and maybe she really was. No more stealing, no more living in fear, no more being stalked by a creepy, twirling ballerina doll.

Kasey walked out of the bus station and into the Memphis sunshine. The sign at a run-down, aqua-colored motel called the Best Choice Inn advertised rooms for $29.99 per night. Kasey seriously doubted it was truly the best choice, but it was better than sleeping on the street, and she had forty bucks in her pocket.

She walked into the motel's dark office and handed a ten and a twenty to a haggard woman in a housecoat and bedroom slippers.

The room had decades-old cheap paneling and once-tan carpet stained by many years' worth of careless guests. But there was a double bed and cable TV and a bathroom that Kasey could have all to herself.

The first step in her fresh start was a shower.

Kasey let the hot water pound her neck and shoulders. She couldn't remember the last time she'd washed her hair, and she used the whole little bottle of motel-issued shampoo to lather up her braids and scalp. She soaped herself from head to toe and let the jets of hot water rinse her clean. It was heaven. Kasey always tried to keep up her hygiene, living on the streets, but there was no way baby wipes and a fast-food restroom sink could compare to a real hot shower.

After she dried off, Kasey brushed her teeth and put on the cleanest clothes she had. It was time to find her fresh start.

Walking the streets of Memphis, she came across an old diner called the Royal Café which had a hand-lettered sign in the window reading HELP WANTED. The café wasn't royal any more than the motel where she was staying was the best choice, but she had to be realistic.

How long had it been since she had worked a real job?

Not since her time at Famous Fried Chicken, where she'd stolen that twenty and started her life of crime.

Inside the Royal Café, a bleached-blonde waitress who could have been anywhere from thirty-five to sixty-five said, "Sit anywhere you want."

"I'm here about the job," Kasey said.

The waitress turned her head and yelled, "Jimmy!"

An olive-skinned man with tired eyes came out of the kitchen, drying his hands on a towel. His apron was stained with grease of various ages. "Yeah?" he said.

"She's here about the job," the waitress said. Her tone implied she didn't think Kasey was a very good candidate.

"You ever bus tables and wash dishes before?" the man, presumably Jimmy, asked.

"Sure," Kasey said. She hadn't, but how hard could it be?

"Them bus pans and dish trays can be pretty heavy. You think you can handle 'em? You're an itty-bitty thing."

"I'm small, but I'm strong."

He smiled a little. "You got a name?"

"Kasey."

"When can you start, Kasey?"

It wasn't a very demanding interview. She hadn't even told him her last name. "When do you need me?"

"How about now?"

It wasn't like she had anything else to do. She might as well start earning money right away. "Sure. But don't I need training or something?"

Jimmy looked at her like she had just asked a stupid question. "You get a bus pan. You clear the dishes from the tables and you put them in the bus pan. You carry the dishes to the kitchen, rinse them in hot water in the sink, then load them in the dishwasher and turn it on. When the dishes are clean, you unload the dishwasher and stack the dishes on the shelves. You got that?"

"Yes, sir."

"Good. That was your training. It's minimum wage, paid in cash at the end of the week. Seven till two Monday through Friday, with one free meal per shift. That okay with you?"

"Yes, sir." The pay was low, but she'd be off work by two, and a free hot meal every day would help her out a lot.

"Good," he said. "Get to work."

The job wasn't so bad. Jimmy yelled a lot, but it was never anything personal. Kasey was able to rent her room in the

Best Choice Inn by the week. She got to take advantage of the laundry room, the shower, and the cable TV, and the one big meal a day at the diner went a long way toward keeping her fed. Plus, Jimmy was a good cook. He said she was too skinny, and his blue plate specials of meatloaf and turkey and dressing were starting to put a little meat on her bones. The work was physically hard but mindless enough that she could daydream about whatever she wanted.

Her only problem at work was that Brenda, the waitress she'd met the first time she walked into the place, seemed to have taken a dislike to her.

"Is that your real name—Kasey?" Brenda asked her one day while Kasey was bussing a table.

"Sure is." She didn't look up, just kept on loading dishes into the pan.

"I was just wondering because you didn't even give Jimmy your last name. He may not have good sense, but I do."

"Is that a fact?" Kasey said, dumping silverware into the bus pan with a clatter.

"You seem shifty to me," Brenda said, looking at her with narrowed eyes. "Like you're hiding something."

"Everybody's hiding something," Kasey said lightly, picking up the heavy tray. "Even if it's just their holey old underwear under their clothes."

She carried the full bus pan back to the kitchen. There was no way Brenda could find out about Kasey's past as a thief. Fortunately, there were no arrest records since she had never been caught. Still, Brenda made Kasey feel like she was being watched, and it was a feeling Kasey didn't like.

One afternoon, when Kasey was bussing tables, she spotted two five-dollar bills lying under the salt and pepper shakers.

The two fives reminded her of that twenty-dollar bill she lifted so easily at Famous Fried Chicken.

Her fingers felt itchy.

Brenda had gone out back for a five-minute break, and Kasey was sure she hadn't seen the money.

In one swift motion, she palmed one five-dollar bill and left the other where it was.

It wasn't really stealing, Kasey decided. It was just splitting the tip fifty-fifty between the person who served the customer and the person who cleaned up after the customer. Cleaning up was harder, too. Customers were messy. Splitting the tip was perfectly fair.

Kasey promised herself she wouldn't make a habit of taking tip money. And she didn't—not really. She only stole when Brenda was on break or looking away, and she never took the whole tip. If a customer left three dollars, Kasey took one. If a customer left seven, Kasey took two. It wasn't much, but it helped with the little things—doing a load of laundry at the motel, buying snacks and soda to have when she watched TV.

And besides, Brenda was always mean to her. Taking a

bit from her tip was like getting paid extra for hazardous duty.

Today Kasey felt unusually hungry when she walked to work. She ignored the fall leaves that swirled near her and left her glasses in her jacket pocket. She willed herself not to think about Ballora but to think about food instead. Usually she took her one free meal per shift at lunch, but today she thought she might order breakfast instead. The Royal Breakfast Special, she decided. Three buttermilk pancakes, two eggs to order, bacon, and home fries. She was running early this morning, so she would have time to eat before the first customers trickled in.

When she walked into the restaurant, Jimmy and Brenda were sitting together in a booth, like they were waiting for her. They did not look happy.

"Kasey, I'm glad you got here early this morning," Jimmy said, gesturing for her to sit down across from them. "We need to talk."

In Kasey's experience, when somebody said *we need to talk*, the words that came after weren't going to be good. Nobody ever said, *"We need to talk. So how about a raise and this plate of warm cookies?"*

With a sinking feeling, Kasey sat down in the booth.

Jimmy folded his hands in front of him. "Brenda has told me that, since you started working here, she's been getting a lot less money in tips. Do you know anything about that?"

The hunger in Kasey's stomach was replaced by fear. "How am I supposed to know what Brenda makes in tips?" she asked.

"Well," Jimmy said, "customers leave their tips on the table, and sometimes the money's still on the table when you bus it, so—"

"I know you've been stealing my tips off the table!" Brenda interrupted. Her face was red with rage. "Not all the money, but enough so you think I won't notice. But I do notice! I know my regular customers. I know what they order, and I know how much they tip."

Kasey remembered the first rule of the Thieves' Den: *If suspected or caught, deny, deny, deny.* "Look, Brenda, I know you didn't like me from the moment I walked in the door. And it's okay. You don't have to like me. But that doesn't mean you have the right to accuse me of things I don't know anything about."

"See?" Brenda elbowed Jimmy. "Shifty, like I said. Aren't you gonna fire her?"

Jimmy closed his eyes and massaged his temples like he had the world's worst headache.

He was quiet so long that Kasey finally broke the silence and said, "Am I being fired, Jimmy?"

Jimmy opened his eyes. "You're not being fired. You're being watched. If there's anything to what Brenda says, cut it out, or you will be fired. Now get back to work."

"Yessir."

"'Cut it out?'" Brenda said. "That's it?"

"Like I said, I'm watching her," Jimmy said, then looked at the door. "Here comes the early-morning crowd. You'd better get to work, too."

On the way home, Kasey walked past a grassy area where the autumn leaves rose and swirled in a circle. *Fine,* she said to herself, and put on the glasses. There was Ballora, spinning nearer than ever. Clearly, there was no getting away from her.

Dizziness overcame Kasey. "Why?" she yelled. "Why do you keep following me?" Several people turned to look at her like she was crazy. Was she crazy? She didn't even know anymore.

That night, Kasey dreamed she was sitting in a red velvet seat in a beautiful theater with a golden domed ceiling. The theater was empty except for Kasey. The lights went down, sending the room into blackness, and orchestral music swelled.

The lights came up on the stage, and Ballora danced out on tiptoe. She danced to the left side of the stage, and a huge purple-and-gold satin banner unrolled from the ceiling. It was printed in fancy letters with the word "*LIAR.*" Ballora put her hands to her cheeks as if startled, then lifted her arms for a long pirouette. She danced over to the right side of the stage, where another large purple-and-gold banner unrolled. This one was printed with the word "*THIEF.*" Ballora put her hands to her cheeks again, then danced to the center of the stage, spun, and looked directly at Kasey. She pointed at her, and one more banner unfurled itself center stage. This one said, *"YOU."*

Kasey woke up gasping, in a cold sweat. She got up, threw on some clothes, yanked open the dresser drawers, and stuck the rest of her clothes in her backpack along with the coffee can of cash she'd saved up from working at the Royal Café. She couldn't go back there. They were onto her. She threw a couple of bills on the nightstand to cover the rest of the rent, then walked toward the bus station.

The fresh air calmed her a little. She shoved her hands in her pockets. There were the glasses. She decided to take one last look. This time, she was really leaving Ballora behind. With a shaking hand, she took them out and put them on.

Ballora was dancing just a few feet away from her. Kasey could see every hinge, every tiny flaw in the paint job. If she walked twenty steps, the two of them would be close enough to touch. Kasey shuddered and took off the glasses.

Okay, I get it, she thought. *I didn't really make a fresh start. I stole, and I lied about it. But if I can just get away—away from her—I really will start over. I'll be a model citizen.*

The next bus out of town was going to Nashville. *Nashville,* Kasey thought. *Why not? A new town, a new job, a new start. For real this time.*

Once she was settled on the bus, Kasey sank into a dreamless sleep.

The Music City Motel, where Kasey rented a room, had the same cheap paneling and stained carpet as the motel in

Memphis, but cost five dollars more a night. Lying on the lumpy mattress, looking at the want ads in the newspaper, Kasey told herself she needed to make a real life. She needed to live instead of just surviving. She needed a job that could give her some kind of future. She needed to make some friends, save up some money, and get that little apartment she'd dreamed of as a kid. Maybe she could go back to school at night and get her diploma. And she could get a dog. She still wanted a dog.

Scanning through the want ads, one caught her eye:

NO EXPERIENCE NECESSARY
OPPORTUNITIES FOR ADVANCEMENT

> Answer incoming calls for a major retail company
> Must be able to communicate well
> Must be able to work in busy, fast-paced environment
> Start at $12 per hour with raises based on merit.
> Open interviews Mon. thru Fri., 9:00 a.m.—2:00 p.m.

It sounded better than washing dishes. But Kasey had nothing to wear to an interview for an office job. She remembered a business communications class she'd taken in high school. The textbook had a whole chapter on how to dress and present yourself for a job interview. Ripped, faded jeans and old boots repaired with duct tape definitely weren't on the list of acceptable apparel.

Kasey got the coffee can from where she'd hidden it in the dresser drawer. She dumped all her money out on the bed and counted it. $229.76. When she set aside what she'd need to pay for the room and the few groceries she bought, that left her with $44.76. Surely she could buy something to wear with that.

She set out on foot in search of a store. She figured the nice clothing stores wouldn't be on this side of town, with its cheap motels and pawn shops and bail bondsman offices. She didn't want to spend any of her meager money on a bus ride to the mall. Besides, she wouldn't be able to afford anything in one of the nice stores anyway.

After an hour of walking, her feet aching in her battered boots, she found a store called Unique Fashions. In the window, bald, white, faceless mannequins modeled colorful dresses. Surely a store in this neighborhood wouldn't be too expensive.

Kasey opened the door and started a little when a bell chimed. She passed a floor-length mirror and saw herself as she must look to other people: her clothes old, baggy, and ill-fitting, her face tired beyond her years. She didn't look like she belonged in this store with its bright lights and neat racks of dresses, tops, and skirts. Maybe she should just go.

"Let me know if there's anything I can help you with, honey," the woman behind the counter said. She was around the age of Kasey's mom, wearing a canary-yellow dress with a bright scarf and perfectly applied makeup.

Kasey wondered if she would ever look so put together. "Thank you," she said.

Kasey browsed through the racks of clothing, not sure what would be best for a job interview, not even sure of what size she wore. Finally, she found a crimson dress splashed with cream-colored flowers. She remembered that once a cute boy in high school had told her red was her color. She knew it would look good on her.

The saleslady who had been at the cash register appeared beside her as if by magic. "Do you want to try that on, honey?"

Kasey nodded. "Trouble is, I've not worn a dress in so long I don't even know what size I wear."

The lady looked her up and down. "Well, you're no bigger than a minute. I'd try a six." She smiled. "It's been a long time since I was a six—about three kids ago! I bet you don't have any of those yet, do you?"

"No, ma'am, not yet." Kasey held on to the dress and tried to imagine a future with a steady job, a comfortable place to live, maybe even a husband and kids. Could that kind of life ever be in the cards for someone like her? It was hard to even picture what it would be like.

"The fitting rooms are over there," the saleslady said. "Just holler if you need anything."

"Thank you." Kasey locked herself in one of the tiny rooms and slipped off her boots, jacket, jeans, and T-shirt. She pulled the dress over her head and looked at herself in the mirror. The saleslady had been right. Kasey was a size six. The dress fit perfectly—not too loose and not too tight—and the crimson-and-cream print complemented her skin tone. She looked respectable. Like a regular person going to a regular job interview.

Except that she had forgotten one thing.

Standing in front of the mirror, Kasey looked at her bare feet, which certainly weren't acceptable in an office job. But neither was wearing battered, taped-up boots with her nice new dress. She had forgotten she'd need shoes, and shoes were expensive.

Feeling discouraged, she took off the dress and put on her ratty old clothes. She carried the dress with her out of the fitting room.

There was a small shoe section in the back of the store. She figured she might as well see how much a pair would cost. There were some decent-looking tan flats in her size on sale for $21.97, but she couldn't afford the shoes and the dress, too, even with the discounted price.

Desperate, panicked, Kasey looked around the store. There were no visible security cameras, and the saleslady was busy helping another customer, an elderly lady trying on a pink suit jacket.

This would be the last time, Kasey promised herself. She was only doing it so she could go to the job interview. She rolled up the dress as small as she could and stuffed it in her backpack. She took a deep breath, grabbed the shoebox with the flats in it, and headed to the cash register.

When the saleslady came to check her out, she said, "Decided not to get the dress?"

"Just these today," Kasey said, handing the saleslady a twenty and a ten. At least she was paying for the shoes and not stealing them, too, Kasey thought. Plus, they would've been difficult to fit in her bag.

The saleslady gave Kasey her change, bagged up the shoebox, and handed it to her. "Thank you, honey. I hope you come back and see us soon."

When Kasey approached the front door, a horrible buzzing sound filled the store. Kasey's stomach knotted in fear. The dress must have some type of anti-theft device on it that activated the alarm. Caught. She'd never been caught before.

"Wait just a second there, honey," the saleslady called. "I must not have scanned those shoes right."

Kasey was about to make a run for it, but outside the front door of the store, hundreds of fall leaves swirled up furiously like a mini tornado. Kasey didn't have to put on the glasses to know that Ballora was right in the center of the tempest. Her heart pounded in her chest.

Kasey knew that if she bolted out the door, she'd run right into Ballora.

She was trapped. One way or the other, she was caught. At least if she stayed in the store, she had some idea of what the consequences would be. If she surrendered herself to Ballora, she had no idea what would happen. She just kept imagining Ballora's long, sharp nails. Her teeth.

The buzzing alarm hurt her ears, making it impossible to think straight.

"Is there a problem, Helen?" Another well-dressed woman, probably the manager, had emerged from the back of the store.

In seconds, the manager and the saleslady were beside Kasey.

"Let me see your bag for just a second," the saleslady said.

Kasey handed it over, hoping they didn't notice how hard she was shaking.

The saleslady showed the manager the receipt. "See, she paid for her purchase."

The manager was looking at Kasey as if she could see every misdeed Kasey had ever committed. "I think we'd better check her backpack, too." She turned to Kasey. "Miss, we need you to open your backpack and let us look inside. If everything checks out, you'll be free to go with our apologies for the inconvenience."

Kasey glanced outside. The leaves were swirling closer and harder, smacking against the glass of the door.

She swallowed hard. There was no choice.

Kasey opened her backpack. The crimson of the dress tucked inside it was as bright as blood.

"That's the dress she tried on!" the saleslady said. She sounded like Kasey's theft was a personal betrayal.

The manager grabbed Kasey's arm. "Well, that's that," she said. "I don't have any choice but to call the police."

Kasey looked outside at the swirling leaves, then back at the stern faces of the two women. Her eyes filled with tears, which was strange because Kasey couldn't remember the last time she had cried. But now she cried for all the things she'd lost, for all the bad things she'd done, and all the good things she'd never gotten to experience.

"Please," Kasey said, sobbing. "Don't call the police. I . . . I need the dress and shoes for a job interview, but I didn't have enough money for both of them."

"So you thought stealing the dress was a good solution to that problem?" The manager was still holding Kasey's arm.

"I knew it wasn't a good solution," Kasey said through her tears. "It was just the only solution I could think of. I'm so sorry." Where were all these tears coming from? It was like she was a human waterfall.

"I have a solution." A voice came from behind them. It was the elderly woman the saleslady had been helping earlier. Her hair was perfectly groomed, and she was dressed elegantly in a cream-colored pants suit. "I'll buy the young lady the dress."

"Mrs. Templeton, we couldn't let you do that," the manager said.

"Of course you can," Mrs. Templeton said. "I spend a lot of money at this store. I'm a good customer, and the customer is always right." She smiled at the manager and saleslady. "Right?"

"Right," the manager said, but she sounded reluctant.

"Good." Mrs. Templeton opened her purse and took out her wallet. "Now there's no need to call the police, and this young lady can get to her job interview."

"What if there isn't a job interview?" the manager said. "What if she's lying?"

Mrs. Templeton looked Kasey up and down. "Well, that's a risk I'm willing to take. But I think she is telling the truth. She has an honest face. She was just in a desperate situation and didn't use her best judgment."

"Thank you," Kasey said, tears still flowing. "I'll pay you back when I can."

"Nonsense." Mrs. Templeton waved off Kasey's offer. "You just help out somebody else when they need it."

Kasey walked out of the store through the swirling leaves.

As she made her way down the street, she was still crying and drawing concerned looks from passersby. She couldn't explain it, but she felt like she was changing, like something hard inside her was softening and breaking up.

She stopped at a park to rest a few minutes. She was tired from all the walking, from all the stress and fear. She sat on a bench, and her hand reached into her pocket for the glasses before she even knew what she was doing. Had she lost Ballora after the woman at the store had made things right?

No. She was right there.

Ballora stood before her and twirled, just a little more than arm's length away. She seemed to stare at Kasey with her blank blue eyes, and then she spun and spun, creating a breeze Kasey could feel on her face. She was close enough to touch.

"Why?" Kasey yelled. "Why can I not get rid of you?" She shoved the glasses in her pocket and ran. She ran away from Ballora even though in her heart she knew Ballora was right there with her. She ran to the Music City Motel and locked the door behind her, panting.

The words of the old woman at the bus station came back to her suddenly: "Sometimes when you try to run away from your problems, those problems end up following you."

Scratch, scratch. The sound was coming from the window. Kasey pulled back the curtain and saw nothing. Then she put on the glasses.

Ballora was pressed against the window. Her face, pretty at a distance, was terrifying up close, split down the middle, with a gaping red mouth and glowing eyes, eyes which Kasey thought saw right into her soul. Ballora's long, blue-painted fingernails scraped against the glass with a horrible metallic screech. Kasey backed away from the window.

"*Okay, Ballora,*" Kasey said. "*Please. Just let me go to this job interview first. Then I know what I have to do.*"

Ballora said nothing, just watched with her glowing blue eyes.

Kasey sat down on the bed and dug around in her backpack until she found what she was looking for: the driver's license of the woman whose purse she had stolen outside of Circus Baby's Pizza World.

Sarah Avery. That was the name on the driver's license. And here, where Kasey was standing in her new crimson dress and tan flats, was Sarah Avery's address. It was a split-level suburban home, not too fancy, but much nicer than anywhere Kasey had ever lived.

It hadn't been easy getting here with no bus fare, but finally Kasey had met a long-haul truck driver who was headed this way and willing to let her ride along. Kasey had slipped on the glasses once during the trip and had seen Ballora's face pressed against the passenger side window, still watching her.

As Kasey stood on the walkway in front of the house, working up the courage to go and ring the doorbell, the fall leaves swirled around her. She didn't put on the glasses, but she felt Ballora behind her, sharing the space in the eye of the tiny tornado. Ballora was close enough to touch, waiting for Kasey to lose her nerve.

Kasey took a deep breath, walked up to the door, and rang the bell. The leaves blew past her with a giant *whoosh*, and Kasey felt a sudden, unfamiliar sense of calm and peace.

A small woman with brown hair opened the door. She was wearing track pants and a T-shirt from a 5K run for charity. "Hello?" she said, sounding a little puzzled.

"Hi." Kasey's voice quavered. "You don't know me, and this is really awkward. Uh . . . do you remember that time a couple of months ago when your purse got stolen outside of Circus Baby's Pizza World?"

"Sure. It was terrible. Nobody forgets something like that." She knitted her brow and looked at Kasey. "Are you . . . the police?"

She was so far off track that Kasey couldn't help but smile. "No, actually, I'm the thief who stole your purse. Ex-thief, that is."

The woman's jaw dropped. "You? But you look so nice. . . . Why did you come here?"

"I came because I wanted to give you this." She pulled Sarah's wallet from her backpack. "I'm sure you've replaced your license by now, but your old one is in there. There's twenty dollars in there, too—my first installment of paying back what I took from you. I have a job now. I start on Monday. I'll send you more money after I get my first paycheck."

Sarah took the wallet. "This is amazing. What made you decide to do this?"

Kasey thought of Ballora spinning wildly. "I guess somebody finally scared me into doing the right thing. I've changed. I mean, I'm still changing. And I wanted to say I'm sorry and ask if you can ever forgive me."

"Of course I can," Sarah said. "So few people admit they've done wrong. It's refreshing to get a real apology. Consider yourself forgiven. As a matter of fact, I was just making some tea. Would you like to come in and have a cup with me?"

"Me?" Kasey said, as though there were somebody else Sarah could be talking to. "Aren't you afraid I'll rob your house or something?"

"As a matter of fact, I'm not. Come in."

Sarah held the door open, and Kasey walked into the bright, sunny house. A big brown dog greeted her, wagging its tail.

In the kitchen, the little girl Kasey remembered from that night was sitting at the table coloring a picture with crayons. She looked first at Kasey, then at her mom. "Mommy, do we know this lady?" she asked.

"No, sweetie, but we're getting to know her," Sarah said, pouring hot water in mugs for tea.

Kasey smiled. In some ways, she felt like she was just getting to know herself. "I'm Kasey," she said to the little girl.

"I'm Isabella," the little girl said. Her eyes were big and blue, but they were bright and lively, not blank like Ballora's.

"Isabella, I think I have something that belongs to you," Kasey said.

Isabella hopped down from her chair. "What is it?"

Kasey reached into her bag, pulled out the cardboard glasses, and held them out to Isabella.

Isabella's wide blue eyes grew even wider. "It's my Ballora glasses! It's my Ballora glasses that got stoled, Mommy!"

Sarah set two mugs of tea and one cup of juice on the

table. "Stolen, not stoled. But you're right. Tell Kasey thank you for returning them."

"Thank you for returning my glasses, Kasey," Isabella said, smiling up at her.

Kasey smiled back. "You're welcome." Kasey knew she didn't need them anymore. And besides, they had always really belonged to Isabella.

Isabella put on the glasses and let out a little gasp of surprise. "There she is!" Isabella said. The little girl stood still for a moment, glasses on, her mouth agape in wonder. And then she started to dance.

COMING HOME

Susie listened to gravel crackling under the tires of her family's old minivan as her mom maneuvered it past Oliver, the big oak tree in front of their house. Susie was the one who named Oliver. Her sister, Samantha, thought naming a tree was stupid. Her parents said it wasn't usually done, but that didn't mean she couldn't do it. So she did.

Oliver was really, really big. Susie's dad said Oliver was older than their house, and that was *really* old. Susie's mom's great-great-great-grandma had been born in this house over 150 years ago, and Oliver was already there.

"As soon as we get the groceries put away," Susie's mom said, "I'll start dinner." She spoke slowly, with weird spaces between some of her words. Susie thought it sounded like someone was trying to stop her mom from talking and her mom was working really hard to talk anyway.

Susie thought of voices as colors. Her mom's used to be

bright orange. Now it was dull brown. It had been this new color for a long time. Susie missed the old color.

"Does spaghetti sound okay?" Susie's mom asked in the same disturbing voice.

Susie didn't respond to the question because she didn't care about dinner, and she knew Samantha *would* care. Samantha cared about everything; she liked to be the boss.

"I think we should have those curlicue noodles instead," Samantha said.

Susie smirked. See?

Samantha's voice had changed colors, too. It had never been bright—her voice used to be kind of a pale blue, but now it was gray.

Susie turned and pressed her nose against the minivan's side window so she could see Oliver more clearly. She frowned. Oliver looked sad, even more than he usually did this time of year. Scattered in a ragged wreath around the base of his thick, knobby trunk, pale yellow and dull red leaves flittered over his exposed roots in the afternoon breeze. More than half of Oliver's branches were bare, including the thick branch that suspended Susie's tire swing. The rest of the branches held leaves the same color as those lying on the ground.

Oliver always lost all his leaves in the fall. Three years before, when Susie was four and Samantha was three, Susie got very upset about the leaves falling from the oak tree. She told her mom the tree was crying. And if the tree was crying, it was feeling bad, and if it was feeling, it needed a name. That's when she named him Oliver. Samantha, though a year younger, said naming a tree was "frivolous." Frivolous was a word she learned from Jeanie, their godmother. Samantha liked learning words. She liked *learning*, period. She didn't like frivolous things the way Susie did.

Susie's mom explained that Oliver wasn't crying when he lost his leaves. He was preparing himself for the winter. He had to let go of the leaves so he could keep his trunk fed through the cold months. Then after the cold months, he'd grow new leaves. "He has to let go before he can regrow," she said. "We all have to do that sometimes."

Susie sort of understood this, but she still thought Oliver was sad. The only thing that made her feel okay about the falling leaves was their beautiful colors. Normally, Oliver's falling leaves were golden yellow and bright red.

As Susie's mom pulled the minivan around the side of the house, Susie turned to look back at Oliver. His leaves looked different this year. Duller and dryer.

Susie wondered if it had something to do with the elves that lived in his trunk. She grinned. She knew Oliver didn't have elves in his trunk; she was just being silly. But she once told Samantha he did, just to bug her.

As soon as the minivan stopped at the stairs to the left of the wraparound porch, Samantha unbuckled her seat belt and threw open her door. Samantha was always in a hurry.

Susie's mom didn't move, even after she turned off the engine. She did this a lot, Susie had noticed. Her mom would kind of get stuck, like she was a windup toy that didn't get wound up enough. She'd just stop in the middle of doing something and stare off into the distance. It scared Susie, because she wasn't sure if her mom was still *there*. It looked like she was, but it felt like she'd left her body behind, a sort of bookmark to hold her place while her thoughts took the rest of her someplace else.

The car engine ticked a few times before going silent. Susie smelled the onions in one of the shopping bags in the back of the minivan. She smelled something else, too. No, not smelled. It wasn't her nose that told her something was in the air. It was . . . what? Her other senses? What senses?

Jeanie once told Susie that she was special, that Susie had an ability most others didn't have. She was "plugged in," Jeanie said. Susie had no idea what that meant, but she liked the sound of it. Jeanie said it was the reason why Susie felt things other people didn't feel. Right now Susie felt like something was wrong. That something was like a smell, like the smell of something . . . rotting? Going stale? Susie wasn't sure.

Susie wanted to say something to get her mom moving again, but then she noticed Samantha was standing next to the minivan, looking through Susie's window. Samantha had that look on her face, the look she often wore lately. Susie didn't understand the look. It was part angry, part sad, and part scared.

Susie's mom finally moved. Sighing, she shook her head and pulled the keys from the ignition. She picked up her purse and opened her door. "We need to get these groceries inside. It could rain."

Susie glanced through the windshield toward the low-hanging gray clouds beyond the steep green roof of the old house. The clouds were heavy and dark.

The big house had a lot of space, so Susie and Samantha each had their own room. Susie, though, liked hanging out in Samantha's room. She thought Samantha would rather she didn't, but even though Samantha liked to boss people around, she wasn't mean. She and Susie both liked people to be happy. So because Susie liked playing in Samantha's room, Samantha let her.

Samantha wasn't as good at sharing other things, though. Like toys. She insisted she and Susie play with their own toys.

Susie always wished she and Samantha could do things together, not just side by side. When Susie got her cool baking set for Christmas a couple years back, the one with all the fun plastic foods and the pots and pans and the hot pink apron, she wanted to play restaurant with Samantha. But Samantha wouldn't do it. She insisted on playing instead with her own construction kit. Even if they were both playing with dolls, Samantha wanted to keep her dolls apart.

Like right now.

Susie sat on the thick blue rug that lay on the floor next to Samantha's big bed. The rug matched the crisp curtains on the window that looked out at Oliver. Susie glanced at him. He looked like he'd dropped a few more leaves. His remaining ones hung limply in the muted gray evening light.

In front of her, Susie's dolls were arranged on blocks set up in a semicircle. It was a choir, and she was going to direct them, but first she had to be sure they were all in their right spots. She moved the dolls around, deciding who would sing what part of the song, humming while she did it. She didn't normally hum—her mother did. But she hadn't heard her mother hum in a long time.

On the opposite side of the rug, Samantha had her own dolls perched in front of boxes. The boxes were "working stations," Samantha said. Susie wasn't sure if the dolls were in school or at a job. Either way, it was pretty clear Samantha's dolls weren't going to have as much fun as Susie's. Did Samantha see that, too? Maybe that was why she kept looking over at Susie's dolls and blocks.

Susie crossed her legs and looked around. Samantha's room was so organized, with light-blue canvas bins stacked up neatly on white shelves, a big white desk with a superbright metal desk lamp, the big bed with its simple metal frame and its perfectly made blue-and-white checked bedspread, the two tidy white nightstands with their small blue lamps, and the window seat covered with its simple thin blue cushion. Susie's room, which she could just see through a connecting door, was filled with color and chaos. She had a window seat, too, thick and tufted and covered in purple velour. It was piled with flowery pillows. Her purple shelves had no bins. Susie hated bins. She liked to see her toys and books and plush animals because they made her feel happy. They all hung out in the open on the shelves, like they were having a big party.

Samantha looked over at Susie's dolls again. She pressed her lips together so tightly it made the skin around her mouth pucker. The expression made her look like an angry Pekinese dog. One of those dogs used to live next door, and the first time Susie saw it, she laughed because it reminded her of Samantha.

Susie wondered if she ever looked like a dog. She didn't think so. Even though she and Samantha had similar hair and basically the same eyes, they didn't look the same on the two girls. Susie's light-brown hair flowed around her face; Samantha's was caught tight in a ponytail. Susie looked wild and mischievous, and Samantha looked like a good girl. Susie's brown eyes were usually wide open, while Samantha's were often squinting, so Susie looked eager and Samantha looked cautious. Susie had a smaller nose and mouth and was usually called cute. Samantha had their dad's larger nose and mouth, and Susie once heard her grandma say about Samantha, "She'll grow into her looks and turn into a handsome woman."

Samantha glanced again at Susie's dolls before rearranging her own dolls to stand at their "stations." Poor things. When Samantha was done with her dolls, they'd have to go back in their bins.

"Do your dolls want to be in my choir?" Susie asked.

Samantha didn't answer.

Susie sniffed. She wrinkled her nose. The air smelled like spaghetti sauce and garlic bread. It also still had that other smell, the one she didn't understand.

Well, fine. She didn't need Samantha's dolls to have a good choir. Making one final adjustment, Susie picked up a ruler and tapped it on the block she had set up in front of her dolls. Then she began waving the ruler back and forth the way she'd seen directors do it.

Before Susie got through three waves, Samantha suddenly stood up and kicked Susie's dolls off their blocks. Then she kicked the blocks, too. All the dolls and blocks tumbled over the fluffy rug and clattered onto the dark wood floor beyond. Susie winced. Now she'd have to set up a hospital with the blocks and heal her dolls.

Samantha glared at Susie before running out of the room. Susie thought about yelling after her, but fighting with Samantha never accomplished anything. She'd learned it was better to be quiet and let things blow over.

Even so . . .

Susie's mom appeared in the doorway. Tall and skinny with dark-brown hair, Susie's mom used to look like she could be a model. Susie remembered when her mom's hair was really shiny and bouncy, when her mom's big eyes were always made up with long fake lashes and her wide mouth was always painted with sassy red lipstick. Now, her mom wore no makeup, and she looked tired. Dressed in faded jeans and a wrinkled blue T-shirt, Susie's mom gazed at the toys on the rug.

Susie got up and walked over to her.

"Mom?"

Her mom kept staring at the toys.

"Are you okay?"

Tears filled her mom's eyes, and Susie felt like someone was squeezing her heart. "I feel like something is wrong," she told her mom. "Something bad has happened, but I don't know what it is."

Susie really wanted her mom to tell her everything was okay, but her mom just covered her mouth with her hand and let the tears spill from her eyes. Susie knew her mom wouldn't answer now. She never liked talking when she cried. And weren't the tears an answer anyway?

Normally, after dinner, her mom would go to the third floor and work. She had a big studio up there because she was a textiles artist, making big modern quilts and woven blankets that people never used on their beds. Her mom's blankets were hung on walls, which Susie thought was weird, but her mom liked making them, and according to her mom, the pretty blankets "paid the bills."

Which was a good thing, because Dad wasn't here anymore. Susie didn't understand why he left. But he was gone. Was that the bad thing?

Susie wrapped her arms around her knees. No. She didn't think so. She thought it was something else.

She wondered if she should try to hug her mom. Probably not. Her mom didn't like to be hugged when she cried.

Susie just stood there, hoping her mom would stop so they could talk. But her mom didn't stop crying. She just pushed away from the doorjamb and walked down the silent hallway.

Samantha was outside, wandering around the front yard and blowing bubbles. Anyone watching her would think she was having fun, but Susie knew Samantha didn't blow bubbles for fun. She did it to study air currents. Susie knew better than to ask if she could blow bubbles, too. Samantha would say no; it would mess up her "research."

But Susie wanted to be near her sister, so she wandered to Oliver, patted him on his rough moist trunk, and ducked inside the faded black tire swing. Pushing off from the ground, she got the swing going, then she threw her head back to look up at the gloomy sky as the swing spun in a lazy circle.

The evening air was cold, but not too cold, and it had that fall scent that Susie had heard others describe as crisp. She didn't know what "crisp" smelled like. She thought fall air was a two-sided smell—tart and musky at the same time. And of course the fall air around her house still had that other smell that she didn't like.

Susie closed her eyes and refreshed her spin. She could hear Samantha trotting around the yard; Oliver's dry leaves crackled under her feet.

Then Susie heard voices. She opened her eyes and turned so she could see the sidewalk.

Long ago, their house was a farmhouse that sat in the middle of lots of land. But as the years went by and all those great-grandmas grew from little girls to old women, the family had to sell part of the land—so said Susie's mom. Eventually, Susie's grandma had sold the last of the land, to someone called a "developer," and the developer built a big subdivision that surrounded the house. The new houses were built to look a little like the old farmhouse—Susie's mom said they were all Victorian. But the new houses didn't have the personality of the old house. The new ones were all in serious colors like gray and tan and cream. Susie's house had lots of fun colors. Mainly it was yellow, but the trim—and there was a lot of trim—was purple, blue, pink, grey, orange, and white. Susie's mom called the trim "gingerbread," which made no sense to Susie because the trim wasn't made of cookies . . . although she wished it was. Susie always thought it looked like her house was dressed up to go out, and the other houses wore everyday work clothes all the time.

The sidewalk in front of the new houses was wide, and it was closer to their house than Susie's mom wanted it to be. Susie didn't mind that. She liked watching people go by, especially from the tire swing. A big laurel hedge along the front of their yard blocked the view of Oliver's lower trunk and the tire swing. Susie liked to stay there and play "spy," watching people through the hedge without them knowing she was there.

The group going by now had five kids in it. She was pretty sure they were in Samantha's class. Three of the kids, all girls, were walking bikes. A fourth kid, a tall boy, was messing around on a skateboard, and the final one, a smaller boy, was on a scooter. It didn't look like he knew exactly how to use it.

"Hurry up, Drew," one of the girls snapped at the small boy.

He was blond, and his hair stuck up all over on his head.

"Yeah," another of the girls said. Both girls had dark hair, and they wore jeans and blue hoodies. "This place is spooky."

Susie slowed the tire swing and listened to the kids. Spooky? Did they sense it, too, that thing that Susie didn't understand?

"Hey, Professor!" the third girl called out. This girl had reddish hair, and her black leather jacket hung open to show a light pink shirt underneath.

Susie knew "professor" was Samantha. Even if the word hadn't been said in a sarcastic tone, Susie knew it was supposed to be an insult. Ever since Samantha started grade school, her classmates had made fun of her for being too serious. Susie hated that the kids did that, and the first time it had happened, she'd tried to stick up for Samantha.

"What's wrong with being smart?" she'd yelled at the kids taunting her sister. "You're just jealous that she knows more than you!"

Susie had thought Samantha would appreciate this support, but Samantha got upset. "I don't need you to take care of me," she told Susie. "I have to stand on my own two feet."

Susie knew Samantha had gotten this expression from their grandma, but she didn't argue. And she never again tried to stop the kids from their teasing.

So she didn't speak up now when one of the girls called out, "Freak!"

"Come *on*, Drew," the boy on the skateboard said to the boy with the scooter.

"I hate passing this house," the leather jacket girl said.

"Yeah," one of the other girls agreed, shivering.

The third girl said, "I used to play with them when I was in kindergarten. She was always serious," she pointed to Samantha, "but she at least would talk to you. Now it's like she's . . ." She shrugged. "I don't know."

The kids had passed the house, but Susie turned to watch them, and she kept listening. "You can't really blame her," the small boy said.

"Come on, Drew," the leather jacket girl said. "Let's just get by, huh?"

When night came, it dropped on the house like someone up in heaven abruptly threw a black blanket over everything. The girls got ready for bed as usual, and as usual Samantha didn't protest when Susie got into her bed. She knew Susie hated to sleep alone.

Even so, Samantha always slept with her back to Susie, and she always slept as far from Susie as possible, especially now. Susie faced the window. Even though the window had a shade, it was never pulled. Susie's mom said the house should have as much light as possible—sunlight or moonlight. Susie liked to lie awake and look at the way the moonlight brought things to life in the room. The eerie glow cast shadows over Samantha's bins, making them look like big mouths trying to gobble the moon. She also liked to look at the stars and name them.

Tonight, the stars were hiding, and only the faintest gleam from the moon's sliver managed to push through the clouds. The only light coming into the room reached dimly from the porch lights over the front and back doors.

The room was cold, and the cold bothered Samantha more than it did Susie. So the girls lay under two thick, soft blankets. Susie shoved the blankets away from her mouth.

"Are you awake?" Susie asked her sister. She kept her voice at a whisper.

Samantha didn't answer. This wasn't unusual. She didn't like talking at night.

But that didn't stop Susie. "I keep having this bad feeling, like something's wrong," Susie whispered. She didn't wait for a response.

"The world smells funny," she told her sister. She twisted up her mouth, trying to describe the smell. "It reminds me a little of when we leave leftovers in a container too long and then Mom tells us to clean them out and we have to hold our nose and talk like this." She held her nose and talked in the funny voice that resulted. She giggled at herself.

Samantha remained silent. She never thought Susie's funny voices were all that funny. And maybe she was actually asleep. Susie held still so Samantha's smooth, blue sheets wouldn't make that shushing sound they made when you shifted in the bed. She focused on Samantha's breathing. It was deep and even.

Susie pulled her legs up tighter and nestled her head further into the pillow. "And Oliver's leaves aren't the right color. They're not bright enough."

Samantha breathed . . . in and out.

"And Mom is acting strange. You know?"

Samantha did not respond.

Susie sighed. She closed her eyes and tried to go to sleep.

Thump.

Susie's eyes shot open.

Had she fallen asleep? Did she dream that muffled sound she just heard?

She lay perfectly still, listening.

Thump . . . thump . . . thump.

No, she didn't dream it. Someone . . . or something . . . was walking around on the porch. The sound was that of a big foot hitting the wooden boards.

Susie sat up, clutching the smooth sheets and Samantha's soft white blankets.

She cocked her head to listen closely. That's when she heard the taps between the thumps.

Thump . . . tap . . . thump . . . tap . . . thump.

Susie didn't move, but suddenly Samantha sat up. She immediately swung her legs over the side of the bed, but she didn't stand. She just sat there, her back rigid.

"You heard it, too," Susie whispered.

Samantha didn't reply, so Susie decided she had to do something on her own. She made herself let go of the covers, then dropped her legs out of the bed. She ignored the cold air that hit her ankles, and she padded out of the room and down the stairs to the kitchen.

Susie paused by the island and looked at the pale yellow glimmer creeping in through the kitchen window. It radiated from the porch light above the back door.

The digital clock over the stove glowed red in the darkened room: 11:50. The refrigerator hummed. The faucet dripped. It had dripped for quite some time, Susie knew—one drip every ten seconds.

She waited through two drips while she listened to the continued thump-tap sequence outside on the porch. When the sounds faded enough to make her think that whatever was making the sound was on the opposite side of the house, she went to the back door, took a deep breath, and opened it.

Just then, Samantha reached over Susie's shoulder and slammed the door.

Susie whirled toward her sister.

Samantha's eyes were huge. Her lips were compressed. And for the first time since she'd said goodnight to their mom, Samantha spoke, "There's nothing out there. Back to bed." She turned and marched out of the kitchen, making it abundantly clear that Susie was supposed to follow her.

Jeanie's voice was so warm and strong that, even though it came through the phone line, it sounded like she was in the room. "You're more than Susie's mom, Patricia," she said.

Patricia held the phone to her ear with one hand while she brushed her limp hair with the other. She sat on the edge of the king-sized bed, the bed that was far too big for her alone. But it had been far too small for her and her husband. That's why he had to leave . . . so they could stop intruding into each other's space. Although why they'd needed all that space was never clear to her.

"And more than Samantha's mom," Jeanie continued. "You're you, and you'll find yourself again. Eventually."

Patricia sighed. "Samantha won't talk to me, except to order me around."

Jeanie laughed. "She's her own woman."

Patricia wasn't sure whether to laugh or cry at that. The idea of her eight-year-old daughter acting like a woman was amusing. But the idea that her daughter had been forced to turn into a pint-sized woman was not amusing at all.

"It will get better," Jeanie said. "It always does."

Patricia nodded even though Jeanie couldn't see her. Jeanie would know she'd nodded.

Patricia and Jeanie had been friends since they were Samantha's age. Together, they'd gone through school, college, and grad school, both in art. When Patricia married Hayden, Jeanie was her maid of honor, and when Patricia had her girls, Jeanie became their godmother. Jeanie was like the sister Patricia never had.

"I don't know if I'm doing this right," Patricia said.

"There is no right," Jeanie said.

That made everything harder somehow.

"I wish . . ." She stopped and froze.

What did she just hear?

Did that come from outside or inside?

"You there?" Jeanie asked.

Patricia stayed silent, listening.

"Patricia?"

Patricia shook her head. She was imagining things.

She blew out air. "I'm here."

Susie had followed her sister back to bed, but now she was creeping away. This time, she paused for a second outside her mom's room. She was probably on the phone with Jeanie. They talked pretty much every day, either in person or over the phone. If Jeanie was in town, she'd come by, but she traveled a lot for her job. Her job was buying art for people. Susie thought that sounded like a very fun job.

Susie lurked in the hallway, hoping to hear her mom laugh. But a laugh never came.

Instead the footsteps sounded again. *Thud . . . tap . . . thud . . . tap.*

Susie put her shoulders back and turned toward the top of the stairs.

Descending slowly, pausing on each step, Susie looked over the top of the waxed oak banister to the paned window at the front of the house. Sheer curtains blurred the outline of the porch rails and beyond them, Oliver's solid presence; he stood like a tireless guard in the middle of the front yard.

But the sheer curtains couldn't block the shape that Susie saw stalking past the windows on the front porch. The shape was too big to hide. All the curtains could do was distort it and disguise what it was.

The shape moved slowly, deliberately, lurching in sync with the sound of its step: *thud . . . tap . . . thud . . . tap.* As it moved, its head swiveled. Every few steps, Susie could see the reflection of sharp eyes as they searched the interior of the house. Every time those eyes looked her way, Susie turned into stone, willing herself to disappear into the background.

Even though she wanted to hide, Susie didn't go back to bed. She couldn't. She knew that.

So she continued down the stairs, managing one step for every six footsteps she heard on the front porch. By the time she reached the first floor, the shape was passing the last of the tall windows on the left side of the house. Susie tiptoed ahead of it.

Ducking into what used to be her dad's office, she watched the shape outside pass the office window and head toward the kitchen side of the house. Hesitating only a moment in the empty room lined with dusty shelves, Susie pushed off the doorjamb and went into the kitchen for the second time that night.

She crouched behind the island as the shape passed through the yellow light outside the kitchen window. Once it had moved on, heading back toward the front of the house, Susie stood. She clenched her fists then released them. And she went to the front door.

The front door was as old as the house. Built of thick wood and stained so many times the door always wanted to stick when you tried to open it, the carved front door reminded Susie that time couldn't be stopped, no matter how much you wanted it to be.

The footsteps paused.

Susie listened. She heard nothing at all.

She reached for the front doorknob, and she opened the door.

She opened the door in increments. Two inches. Six inches. A foot. She took a deep breath, stepped around the door . . . and looked up.

She waited. Like she always did. Every night. Frightening. Familiar. Persistent.

Susie didn't cringe or tremble or jump back, even though it would have been reasonable for her to do any or all of those things. Instead, she said, "Is it time to go back already?"

Chica held out her yellow hand. Her mouth didn't move.

Susie knew Chica wouldn't answer, because Chica didn't talk to her.

Susie turned away from the man-sized animatronic chick standing in front of her. She looked back up the stairs. Longing.

But longing didn't do any good.

Susie looked back to the animatronic chick. Ignoring the gaping metal mouth with all the teeth, Susie focused on Chica's bright yellow body and the big white bib hanging around Chica's neck, the one that said, "Let's Eat!" Then she looked at the cupcake Chica held. Susie thought the cupcake was scarier than Chica. It had eyes and two buck teeth, and one candle stood up straight from the middle of it. Susie didn't know what the candle was for. One day? One year? One child?

Letting Chica take her hand, Susie walked away from her house. Every step made her feel less like herself. By the time she passed Oliver's still-falling leaves, she was lost.

Patricia stared through the open front door at the oak tree that was dropping its leaves all over the front lawn. She had a feeling she'd just missed something important.

Several minutes before, she'd heard the sound again. This time, she couldn't talk herself out of it.

She'd left her bedroom and come out into the hallway. When she'd looked down the stairs, the front door was standing wide open.

Heart racing, she'd run to Samantha's room and peered in. One glance slowed her heart rate. Okay. Her worst nightmare wasn't playing out.

But why was the door open? Grabbing a pair of knitting needles and holding them in front of her like a knife, she crept through the house, checking for an intruder. There was nothing.

Patricia closed the door, turned the deadbolt, and pressed her hands against the door, pushing with all her strength as if she could shove away reality, maybe press it into some other form.

Pulling her hands back abruptly, sucked in her breath. There was something she hadn't considered. What if someone had come through the still-open door while she searched the house?

She turned and ran up the stairs to Samantha's room.

She nearly collapsed in relief. Everything was okay.

Samantha was awake. She sat up in bed, the covers pulled up to her neck, her fists clenched and her knuckles stark white. Tears made her eyes sparkle in the faint light from her bedside lamp.

Patricia sat down next to her daughter. She wanted to

pull Samantha into a tight hug, a never-let-you-go hug. But Samantha wouldn't like that. All she tolerated was the slightest touch.

So Patricia briefly placed her hand on Samantha's shoulder before she said, "I know you miss her. I miss her, too."

Samantha blinked and two tears escaped her eyes, meandering down her lean cheeks. She didn't bother to wipe them away.

Patricia sat next to Samantha for a long time, but neither mother nor daughter spoke again. Finally, Patricia stood, kissed the top of her daughter's head, and returned to her huge bed.

Samantha waited for her mother to leave before she moved. She lay on her back watching the light and shadow play cat and mouse on her ceiling.

If Susie was here, she'd make up some story about the shadows and light, about them fighting each other or dancing or something. She was always making up things.

Susie got that from their dad. Even though their mom was the artist, and their dad was the one who went to work in a suit and tie and did stuff for "business" that neither Samantha nor Susie understood, he was the one who loved stories. In his free time, he was always either reading a book or watching a movie. He could make up good stories, too. When he was home, the girls had always had an original story at bedtime. Their mom wouldn't even try to make up a story. "I'll read you a story instead," she would say when their dad was out of town. Now she didn't say, "instead." She just asked what book she was reading tonight.

One of the stories their dad made up was about a little boy who had a secret place in a hidden room in his house. From that room, he was able to solve all his problems, no matter what they were. He told hundreds of these stories, making up a new problem for the boy to solve each time.

Susie was convinced these stories meant there was a secret room in their house. She was always asking their dad about it. His answer was always the same; he'd pretend to zip his lips shut and throw away an invisible key.

Susie said she thought the way to the secret room was in their dad's office at the back of the house. Samantha thought it was just a story, and she was glad the office was always locked so Susie couldn't talk her into getting in trouble looking for the secret room.

Now, the office wasn't locked because her dad was gone. But Susie no longer talked about looking for a secret room.

Samantha pressed her lips together, disgusted with herself for thinking about Susie and the stupid secret room. Then she thought about the sounds she heard at night. She tried to convince herself she imagined them. That had to be true, because when she looked outside, she never saw anything at all.

But lying here alone in the silence, in the strange halfway land of the night, she couldn't quite convince herself that she'd made it all up.

She was pretty sure something had been outside.

But what?

And why?

In the brisk late-morning air, Patricia and Jeanie sat side by side in the porch swing padded with yellow floral cushions. Patricia was aware that, to any passersby, she and Jeanie were part of an idyllic scene: both women, wearing wide-brimmed straw hats to shade their faces from the sun that slanted onto the porch, sipped tea to ward off the fall chill. They probably looked as relaxed as could be. They weren't. Or at least Patricia wasn't.

Patricia studied her friend. Jeanie was almost her perfect opposite in size and coloring. Whereas Patricia was tall and thin with dark hair, Jeanie was short and plump with blonde hair. In spite of these differences, both women used to have one quality in common—they both smiled and laughed easily. Now, Patricia couldn't do that anymore.

Patricia took a shaky breath. "I'm wondering if I should take Samantha to a different counselor." She cringed at the way her voice seemed to scar the air. "Rhonda is nice, and Samantha likes her, I think—honestly, it's hard to tell." She waved away a fly. "But I talked to Rhonda last week, and she says Samantha's stuck. Samantha is clearly keeping something to herself, but nothing Rhonda is doing will get her to talk."

"Samantha has always done things in her own way," Jeanie pointed out. She grinned. "That child has an opinion about everything."

Patricia attempted a smile but only got about halfway there.

"Remember how she harangued Susie relentlessly about naming that tree?" Jeanie gestured at the ancient oak. "What's his name?"

"Oliver." Patricia started crying.

Jeanie set down her tea and took Patricia's hand. "I'm sorry. That was insensitive."

Patricia wiped her eyes and shook her head. "It's been a year. I should . . ."

"There aren't any *shoulds* when it comes to losing a child. Isn't that what your counselor told you?"

Patricia nodded. "No rule book."

They sipped tea in silence for several minutes. Patricia watched Oliver drop another dozen leaves. The previous night's persistent breeze had taken hundreds of Oliver's remaining leaves. He didn't have many left on his gnarled branches. Pretty soon, he'd need his scarf.

Jeanie patted Patricia's knee. "You're thinking about Oliver's scarf."

It made Patricia literally ache to think about how four-year-old Susie had run inside after Oliver had dropped his last leaf that first year she named him. When she'd returned, she held one of the neck scarves Jeanie had knitted for her.

Patricia gazed at Oliver and felt like she could see the scene from three years before unfolding in front of her now. The scene was a little fuzzy in places, but otherwise it was almost real.

Her little arms crossed, her brow furrowed, Susie said, "He'll get cold 'cause he doesn't have leaves." She was dressed in her bright-orange jacket.

When Susie found out the scarf wasn't big enough for Oliver, she was heartbroken... until Patricia suggested Susie ask her godmother to knit a scarf specifically for Oliver. Now, Jeanie knitted a new scarf for Oliver every year.

"I've already knitted it," Jeanie whispered.

Tears spilled down Patricia's cheeks. She was surprised she still had tears to cry. "She was always anthropomorphizing," Patricia said. "I never saw a problem with it."

"There wasn't a problem with it. She was an empathetic child with a vivid imagination."

"Which is why she was so easily lured..." Patricia didn't recognize her own voice. Normally soft, it was now as hard and rough as Oliver's bark. "I should have discouraged her flights of fancy. I should have—"

"Stop it!" Jeanie shifted to face Patricia. "Not all the murdered children were like Susie. You don't know that it would have been different if she'd been a different kind of child. You can't keep trying to find reasons to blame yourself."

Patricia looked down. "I hated that place," she whispered. "It always seemed creepy to me. But Susie loved it."

Jeanie frowned. "Are you sure you want to go over this again?"

"I need to—"

"No, you don't."

"Yes, I do. I can't just forget."

"Why not? How are you helping Susie by torturing yourself with the details over and over?"

Patricia wanted to yell at Jeanie to shut up, but she didn't have the energy.

Jeanie took both of Patricia's hands. "Your daughter was murdered by a serial killer. She was lured to her death in a place where she should have been safe. There. We've dug it up again. Feel better?"

Patricia yanked her hands back and started to stand. Jeanie grabbed her arm and held her in place, her grip pinching Patricia's skin.

"Don't run away!" Jeanie shouted. Then she lowered her voice but kept it firm, just shy of scolding. "You can't dredge up the past and then run from it. If you insist on trotting it out to torture yourself regularly, at least you should do it head-on. If you don't, you'll be running away your whole life, and you'll never be able to let Susie go."

A car zipped by on the road, its engine revving. The smell of exhaust wafted up to the porch. Something about the odor erased Patricia's anger.

"She was wearing her favorite sweater, the one you knitted for her."

"Magenta with pink stripes," Jeanie said.

"She wanted sequins," Patricia said.

"And you wouldn't let me put any on the sweater."

"So you put rhinestones on her jeans instead."

Jeanie laughed. "You were really angry with me."

Patricia wiped her eyes. "Stupid thing to be angry about."

Jeanie gently squeezed Patricia's arm then let her go.

A breeze curled up onto the porch from the yard, and Patricia shivered.

Susie watched Samantha lean on a rake and scowl at Oliver.

"It's not his fault," Susie said. "He can't help it that his leaves land on the ground when he lets them go."

Samantha sighed.

Susie tried not to be annoyed. "I said I'd do it," she reminded Samantha.

Right after they'd gotten home that afternoon, their mom said, "Maybe you can do a little raking before dinner."

Susie had said, "I'll do it."

But before Susie could get to the rake, Samantha grabbed it, and now she wouldn't let go. She'd rather "do it right" and not like doing it than let someone else do it "wrong."

Fine. Let Samantha rake. Susie would hang out with Oliver.

Listening to the rasp and scuff of the rake, Susie went around to the back side of his trunk, away from the road, and hugged him. Oliver smelled smoky and moist. Laying the side of her face against his trunk, she listened. Sometimes when she listened really hard, she was sure she could hear him breathing.

"Hi, Samantha!"

The greeting came from the sidewalk. Susie peered

around Oliver to see who was calling out to her sister. It was Drew, the kid with the scooter and the blond spiky hair. Today he was alone.

Holding on to his scooter, Drew looked across the yard. Samantha stared back at him as if he was a bull about to charge her.

Drew waved. "I see you at school a lot, and I just thought I'd say hi. I'm Drew."

Samantha glanced around like she suspected a trap. Susie wanted to go to her side and encourage her to talk to the kid, but Samantha would hate that. So Susie stayed hidden and watched.

Drew scratched his nose, and his scooter fell over. He bent to pick it up.

"Hi," Samantha said.

Drew straightened and grinned.

Samantha held the rake like a weapon. Susie didn't think that looked very friendly.

"Go over to him," Susie hissed at her sister.

Samantha ignored her. Susie knew listening to someone else's conversation was "rude," according to her mother. So she ran over to the side yard and started talking to the bedraggled plants in the flower beds. Would they tell her why her mom was ignoring them?

Samantha wished the boy would go away. She also hoped he would stay. He was cute.

But was he being nice or just messing around with her?

Drew stepped closer so he was right at the edge of the sidewalk. "Um, I was really sorry about what happened to your sister."

Samantha looked down, but she managed to mumble, "Thank you." She took a tentative step toward the sidewalk.

Drew looked at Samantha. Then he looked up at the house. He lowered his voice. "Do you ever see her?"

Samantha went still. She felt the blood rush from her face, and she gripped the rake so hard it hurt.

Drew dropped his scooter and took several steps into the yard. Then he opened his mouth and words tumbled out so fast they piled up on each other. "I'm not trying to be mean, and I'm not making fun. Really. It's just that I believe in ghosts, and I think people who die can stay around if they want. I had an uncle who died, and I saw him the night he died, and then he came back for a couple years after that. He was waiting for my dad to forgive him for something. I think ghosts hang around if they want something, you know? So I was just asking, and I didn't mean to upset you."

"Dinner's ready in five," Samantha's mom called from the porch. She didn't notice Drew.

Samantha had no idea what to say, so she just said, "Okay," then turned around to head inside.

"Bye," Drew called.

Samantha couldn't go to sleep because she kept thinking about Drew. About what he'd said. Thinking about Drew was kind of nice. Thinking about what he said was not.

His words bounced around in her head. "Ghosts hang around if they want something."

A faint snick and swish sound came from downstairs.

Samantha sat up. She knew exactly what that sound was. Should she go down? Or wait?

The tremors that always started at that sound began at her feet and scrabbled up her legs. Ignoring them, she jumped out of bed and padded across her room and into the hall. No sound came from her mom's room. Nothing from downstairs now, either. But was that a cold draft?

Samantha clenched her jaw and forced herself down the stairs. At the bottom, she paused, then she tiptoed through the dining room and peered into the kitchen.

As she knew it would be, the back door was standing wide open. And now she could hear the other noise, coming from the porch: *thud . . . tap . . . thud . . . tap.*

Moaning, she pushed through her terror. She ran through the kitchen, and she slammed and locked the back door. Then she sprinted as fast as she could back up to her bed.

Once there, she tried to convince herself she was making everything up.

In all the months she had been seeing her, Rhonda had never put her back to Samantha before. Was this some kind of test?

Samantha frowned and tried to figure out what was

going on. She looked around the room. It was plain and neat, the kind of room Samantha liked. All it had in it was a thick tan rug, Rhonda's listening chair—a cream-colored plush chair with a low back and fat arms—a tan-and-cream striped sofa, and a child-sized wood table next to a trunk filled with toys. The room was interesting to Samantha because it extended out from the house, like a box, hovering about two feet off the ground. Three of the box's sides were glass.

A long sigh from Rhonda made Samantha blink, and Rhonda finally swiveled back to face her.

"I'm sorry," Rhonda said. "I've been trying to figure something out."

The crinkle between her thick black brows was unusual. Rhonda didn't frown. Mostly, she smiled too much, in Samantha's opinion. It wasn't normal, especially for someone who listened to other people's problems all day.

"I like figuring things out," Samantha said.

"I know you do." Rhonda brushed back her long black hair.

Samantha stared at Rhonda's big brown eyes. "So what are you trying to figure out?" she asked.

"I'm trying to figure out how to keep your mom from sending you to someone else."

Samantha jerked her head up. "Why does my mom want to send me someplace else?"

"Because you're not making progress with me."

"What's that mean?"

Rhonda leaned forward. "Samantha, I know something is stuck in your head. A thought. A belief. Something you keep thinking is trapped there, in your brain, and you're not letting it out."

Rhonda was right, but Samantha didn't tell her that.

Samantha stared at her neatly tied navy blue sneakers. She liked things to be in their right places. She didn't like messy.

Change was messy. Therapy was messy, too. Before she'd started seeing Rhonda, her mom had taken her to two other people who were "there to help her." Both had wanted her to play with a messy pile of toys in a messy room. She'd begged her mom not to make her go back.

Finally, her mom brought her here. She didn't love it here, but she didn't hate it, either. Rhonda was different. This room was different. Samantha was okay with them both.

"We had a fight," she said.

She had to tell Rhonda what was stuck so her mom wouldn't make her go someplace else.

"You and Susie?"

Samantha nodded.

"Okay." Rhonda scribbled on her notepad. That used to bug Samantha—the scribbling—but she'd gotten used to it.

"It was about Gretchen."

"Who's Gretchen?"

"The doll my mom said we had to share."

"Whose doll was it?"

"Mom gave it to both of us, together." Samantha rolled

her eyes. "I hated that. I want mine to be mine. I don't take Susie's stuff, so I should have my own stuff."

"Okay."

"But Mom said we had to share."

Rhonda nodded.

"So I tried to explain to Susie that we should each get Gretchen for a certain time. When Gretchen was with me, she'd study."

Rhonda smiled and nodded again.

"Susie got upset about that. She said Gretchen didn't like to study. Gretchen liked to go to the zoo. She wanted Gretchen to hang out with her stuffed animals all the time. She said if Gretchen had to study, she'd be sad."

Samantha stopped and remembered Susie standing in her room, hands on her hips, her lower lip jutted out. When Samantha insisted that Gretchen needed to study, Susie threw a tantrum. She cried, "But she'll *hate* that!"

"So what happened?" Rhonda asked.

Samantha swung her legs. "When I tried to put Gretchen in front of a book, Susie grabbed her and ran off. She . . ."

"She what?"

Samantha counted her breaths the way Rhonda taught her. It was supposed to help with the feeling that bugs were crawling up her legs.

One.

Two.

Three.

Four.

On the fourth exhale, Samantha said, "She ran away and hid Gretchen. Then she came back and told me what she'd done. I told her I'd find Gretchen, and Susie was upset again. Before . . . that night . . . she told me she was going to find a better hiding place for Gretchen, and I'd never find her now." Samantha fisted her hands and held them in front of her face.

Then she said, "I think she was thinking about where to hide Gretchen, and that's why she got taken. She thought whoever took her would help her hide the stupid doll."

Rhonda took a deep breath. "Thank you for telling me."

"Am I not stuck anymore?"

"I don't think you are."

Samantha nodded once. Good.

"Where is the doll now?" Rhonda asked.

"I haven't found it."

Susie thought Samantha was unusually talkative today. She hadn't shut up since their mom had picked her up from the funny glass house Samantha visited three times a week. Even though Samantha was talking about boring stuff, about multiplying and dividing fives, their mom seemed to be okay with listening. She kept nodding as she drove through traffic. She didn't smile, though. Neither did Samantha. Samantha was so stiff she looked like a robot. She sounded like a robot, too. It was weird. She was talking as if she had to talk or something bad would happen.

If she had to talk, couldn't she talk about something good?

"How about we talk about cute things?" Susie asked.

Samantha and her mom must not have heard her because Samantha kept talking about numbers and math. Susie sighed.

What was the point in hanging out with them if they were going to ignore her?

Susie turned and looked at Samantha's right ear. Samantha's ears weren't pierced like Susie's were. Susie liked to wear pretty-colored earrings. Samantha refused to have hers pierced because she didn't want holes in her ears. Susie wondered, *if I blow hard enough, can I push all the boring words out of her head?*

Turning, Susie blew as hard as she could into Samantha's ear.

Samantha stopped talking.

Ha! Susie grinned.

"Were you done with your story?" Susie's mom asked Samantha.

Samantha didn't answer. She sat perfectly still in her seat.

Susie wasn't sure the silence was any better than the nonstop chatter. It wasn't a soft, comfortable silence, like a cushy plush bear. It was a sharp silence, like the pointy ends of metal things poking at your skin. The silence hurt her ears . . . and her heart.

Susie started singing to drown out the silence. No one

sang with her, but she didn't care. She sang until Susie's mom turned onto their road. Then Susie stopped and waited eagerly to spot her house and check on Oliver.

Susie's mom paused to wait for a car to pass before turning into their driveway. The car's blinker did its click-tick until Susie's mom made the turn. Susie mimicked the noise. No one told her to stop.

Oliver had lost a lot more leaves. He only had a few left. Would they last long enough?

Susie sat on the end of Samantha's bed and watched her sister read a book. Samantha seemed tense. She held the book stiffly, and she took a long time to turn the pages.

"I have a confession," Susie said.

Samantha didn't look up.

"I miss you guys when we're apart. And I know you miss me, too."

Samantha turned a page. Her hand trembled.

"And I miss Gretchen. Do you miss her?"

Samantha kept reading.

Susie never liked it when Samantha ignored her, but she didn't let it shut her up. "I don't know why, but I can't remember where I hid Gretchen." Susie chewed on a knuckle. "I don't think . . ."

She stopped talking. This wasn't working. Samantha wasn't going to help her.

Why couldn't Susie remember where she hid Gretchen?

She remembered how angry and upset she was that

Samantha was going to make Gretchen study. Gretchen was a sensitive doll. Freckled and curly-blonde-haired, Gretchen's soft round face was painted with a shy smile, the kind of smile that told Susie that she was easily scared. When Susie hid Gretchen, she'd been wearing a pink-and-purple polka-dot dress that Jeanie made. The dress was supposed to be fun. It was supposed to help Gretchen be happier.

But then Samantha was going to put pressure on Gretchen to "learn stuff." Not even polka dots could win out over that.

Susie knew that Gretchen still needed to be with her. Susie was the only person who understood her. She knew what it was like to want to be happy and have fun in a world that wanted you to learn and keep getting better at things. She couldn't leave Gretchen alone, lost in some forgotten hiding spot. She wished Samantha would listen. Susie reached over the book Samantha was holding. She waved her hand around.

Samantha's face got white, and she held very still. *What was she thinking?* Susie wondered. She would've asked, but she knew Samantha wouldn't answer her.

Sometimes Samantha acted like this and sometimes Samantha acted normal. Their grandma used to say, "That Samantha—she's a hard child to read. But Susie is an open book." If Susie was so open, why couldn't Samantha get what Susie was trying to tell her?

How could Susie make Samantha understand?

Samantha leaped out of bed and put her book neatly on

the corner of her desk. Sitting in her straight-backed white desk chair, she opened a drawer and pulled out construction paper and crayons.

That was it! Maybe Susie could draw a picture. Samantha would see it and remember Gretchen.

Or maybe if Susie drew a picture, *she'd* remember where she'd hidden Gretchen.

Susie stared at the paper and crayons. Would Samantha share?

"Samantha, could you come here, please?" their mother called.

Perfect. Susie waited for Samantha to leave the room, and then she stole a pink piece of paper and a purple crayon that had barely been used. She plunked herself down on Samantha's blue rug and stretched out on her stomach. Tucking her tongue firmly between her lips, Susie started drawing. It took all of her concentration to make sure the drawing showed up on the page, but it did.

Drawing was all she could do. If she wrote a note, Samantha wouldn't read it.

"Don't draw too long," Susie's mom said, out in the hallway. "I'll be in to tuck you in soon."

Susie heard Samantha's footsteps coming. She hurried to finish her drawing. When she was done, she left it lying on the floor and retreated to the window seat.

Tucking herself into a small ball, Susie looked out the window. She couldn't see Oliver because the window reflected Samantha's bright room. She could see, though, a couple of leaves pushing against the window. Leaning forward, she realized that they belonged to Ivy, the vine that climbed up the trellis above the porch roof.

Susie smiled. She remembered when her dad had put that trellis on the house. Her mom's ivy, which Susie had named Ivy, of course, had climbed up the porch posts at the front of the house, and her mom had wanted to cut it. Susie thought that would be sad. "Can't you let Ivy climb higher?" she'd asked.

Her mom said, "Well, if we had a trellis . . ."

Now it looked like Ivy had reached the top of the trellis and was trying to climb into Samantha's room. Would Ivy have better luck getting Samantha to talk?

Samantha burst into her room and headed toward her desk. If she wanted to finish her drawing tonight, she'd have to hurry.

Before she reached her desk, though, Samantha noticed something on the floor. Nothing besides the rug was supposed to be on the floor. But a piece of pink paper lay on it. The paper hadn't been there when she left the room. She was sure of it.

Her mom had been with her downstairs, the whole time. No one else was in the house.

That meant . . .

Samantha didn't want to look. If she looked . . .

No longer in a hurry to draw, Samantha stared at the pink paper for a very long time.

Eventually, she convinced herself that picking it up was better than letting it lie there. As long as it was on the floor, Samantha could come up with all kinds of scary reasons for it to be there. If she picked it up, she'd know what it was for sure.

Susie always thought Samantha didn't have much imagination. That wasn't true. The problem was Samantha had way too much imagination. She had so much imagination that she could scare herself silly with just a thought or two.

Taking slow, quiet steps, Samantha walked toward the rug. She didn't take her eyes off the paper as she walked. She couldn't have said why. Did she think it was going to leap off the floor and attack her? And do what? Give her paper cuts?

Samantha had gotten one of those when she was little. Susie had cried when she saw the blood. Samantha didn't. Yes, it stung a little, but she thought it was more interesting than painful. How could something as flimsy as paper cut you?

When Samantha picked up the paper, she saw some squiggly purple lines. But as she gazed at the paper and the squiggly lines, they began to form into shapes that made some kind of sense.

The drawing had three parts, like the panels in newspaper comics.

The first part, on the far left of the page, was a drawing of two little girls. One had a ponytail, and one had hair that was flying all around her face. The flying-haired girl held what looked like a mirror in one hand. She extended the mirror out toward what seemed to be a baby floating in the air. The other hand was held out to the pony-tailed girl. Between the baby and the girl, a big chick with spiky teeth held up its hands. Huh?

The second part of the drawing, which was separated from the first part by a vertical line, showed the moon over a house that looked a little like Samantha's house. The flying-haired girl was walking away from the house, holding hands with that same big chick. To the right of this second drawing, another vertical line separated the second drawing from a third one. The third one also had a moon, a house, and the flying-haired girl walking away hand-in-hand with the chick. But after the third drawing there was a heavy dark line. Samantha could see where the crayon had been moved over and over until it created a thick slashing shape that Samantha didn't understand.

Frowning, she stared at the picture. Had she drawn it and then forgotten?

If only she could believe that.

"I wish you would just talk to me," Susie whispered. "I miss when we used to talk. I know you thought I talked too much, but you still listened. I'd really like someone to listen."

She was so frustrated. This reminded her of playing charades. Once, she'd played charades at her friend Chloe's birthday party. Susie liked all games, but charades wasn't as fun as she wanted it to be. She'd thought she was being so clear with her acted-out clues, but no one got what she was trying to make them see. No one guessed right. When she told her mom about it later, her mom said, "You don't think the same way other people do. That's a good thing. You're super-creative."

Not creative enough, Susie thought as she stared at the drawing she'd left on the rug.

What else could she do?

Jumping up from the window seat, Susie ran to Samantha's desk. She noticed Samantha looked up from the pink and purple drawing when she rushed past, but Susie didn't bother to say anything. When Samantha was acting like this, there was no point. Besides, Susie wanted to draw something else.

At Samantha's desk, Susie grabbed a piece of pale yellow paper and a black crayon. She plopped down in Samantha's desk chair, and started again.

Samantha had felt the air shift, but she didn't want to think about why it shifted. She also knew, somehow, that she couldn't turn around.

Samantha covered her mouth with her hand so she wouldn't giggle. Samantha wasn't normally a giggler. Well, sometimes, her dad could get her to giggle by tickling her. But this wasn't a tickle-giggle. This giggle came from some terrified place inside of her, a place where she was "hysterical." That was a word her dad often used for her mother before he left them all. Samantha didn't want to be hysterical.

She counted her breaths like she did in therapy.

One.

Two.

Three.

Four.

The air in Samantha's room had become thick and sticky, like molasses. Samantha didn't know what would make air feel like molasses, but it didn't feel right to be inside of air like that. She had to get out of here.

Leaving the drawing where she found it, she started to run from the room. But at the doorway, she stopped. Something was lying on her desk.

Another drawing.

Samantha winced and shrank away, but she couldn't remove her gaze.

Like the first drawing, this one had three boxes. In the first, the same flying-haired girl was walking away from the front door of the same house. The moon was a thin sliver, kind of like the moon Samantha had seen the previous night. In the second box, the same girl was walking away from the same door, but the moon was a bigger sliver. And then, in the third box, the girl wasn't even there. This box just showed the house's door and an even bigger moon.

"Are you ready for bed?" Samantha's mom called.

Ignoring the weird air in the room, Samantha gathered

the drawings and shoved them under her covers. She'd look at them later, by flashlight.

Susie usually waited until their mom left to crawl into bed with her sister, but tonight was different. She didn't want to waste a second being apart.

Curling up on the window side of Samantha's bed, Susie watched Samantha go through her funny bedtime ritual.

First, Samantha had to sit at her desk and write a paragraph, at least a paragraph, in her diary. Then she had to go across the hall to the bathroom and brush her teeth. Then she had to pee, and then she had to drink half a glass of water. "That will just make you have to pee again," Susie had told her sister one night. Samantha just stuck out her tongue.

After the water, Samantha touched her toes four times, and she brushed her hair fifty times. Then she went to her doll bin and said goodnight to her dolls. Then she got in bed.

None of these things were funny by themselves, but the way Samantha did them all the same way every night, in the same order, *was* funny. At least to Susie.

Tonight, the routine was a tiny bit different because Samantha got her small flashlight from her nightstand drawer. When Samantha slid under the covers, she pushed the flashlight under the covers with the drawings she'd stuffed under there, and the drawings crinkled. Susie listened to them rustle as Samantha shoved them further down and then arranged herself sort of like a sleeping princess. Finally, she called out, "I'm ready, Mom."

Susie studied Samantha's profile while they waited for their mom to come into the room. Samantha had a little bump on her nose about halfway up from the rounded tip. Susie liked that bump. Susie didn't have a bump, and she thought bumps made noses interesting. She also liked the little check mark–shaped scar under Samantha's right eye. Susie *did* have a scar, but hers was hidden under the hair at the top of her forehead.

Susie got her scar because she was doing something she wasn't supposed to do. Samantha got her scar because Susie was doing something she wasn't supposed to do.

Susie loved to climb on things when she was little. One of her favorite things to do was get up on the porch rail and try to walk all the way around the house on it. She was good at balancing on the rail, but climbing around the posts that held it up could be hard because her arms were too short to wrap around them. She fell a lot, usually landing in her mom's flower beds and getting in trouble. Their mom was super-serious about her flowers.

One day, while Susie was brushing off the dirt from her latest fall, Samantha said, "There's a better way to get around the posts."

"Who says?"

"I say."

"How do you know?"

"I just do, and I know how to do it, too."

"Okay, then show me," Susie said.

"No. Mom said not to get up there."

"Well, then why did you say that?"

"Because there's a better way."

"But if you're not going to show it to me, who cares if there's a better way? You're just being a know-it-all."

"Am not."

"Are too."

The girls faced off next to the yellow begonias at the side of the house. Hands on hips, they glared at each other, practically nose-to-nose. Even though Susie was a year older, she wasn't any taller than her sister.

"I think you're lying about a better way," Susie said.

"I'm not lying."

"Yes, you are."

"No, I'm not."

By now, they were yelling.

"What are you girls fighting about?" their mom called.

She was inside the house doing laundry, and Susie wanted her to stay there so they could keep playing. She leaned toward Samantha until they touched noses, and she whispered, "Yes, you are."

Samantha made her Pekinese face and said, "Fine." Then she marched around Susie and climbed up onto the railing next to one of the posts.

Susie's mouth dropped open.

Samantha put her back to the post. "See, you have to go around it facing out, not facing in. That way, the weight of your butt doesn't pull you off the railing."

Samantha started to demonstrate, but her foot slipped. She lost her grip and fell forward off the railing and into the flower bed. Susie had fallen there before and just gotten dirty, but somehow Samantha's face struck the top of one of the stakes holding up their mom's clematis.

Samantha was mad at Susie for days after that, not only because she had to have stitches but because she got in just as much trouble for being on the railing. "It was her idea!" Samantha had yelled, pointing at Susie.

"You know better than that," their mother said to Samantha. "You don't do anything you don't want to do."

She was right about that.

Like now.

"Not that story," Samantha was saying to their mom. "I want you to read the one about the happy ghost."

Susie smiled. This had become Samantha's favorite story lately.

Susie's mom looked like she was going to argue, but then she sighed and picked up the top book from the neat pile on Samantha's nightstand. Susie's mom sat on the edge of the bed.

Susie wished she could do something for her mom. She looked so pale . . . no, more than pale. She looked like her skin was turning invisible. Susie could see her mom's veins crawling over her forehead and up her hands and arms. They looked like blue worms.

The first time Susie had seen veins like that on an old

lady, she'd thought they *were* worms, and she'd screamed. Her mom had explained what the blue jagged lines were.

"In a tall, old house, on top of a tall, old mountain, the tall, old ghost floated through the main hall," Susie's mom began reading.

Susie plumped the pillow under her head, and scooted closer to Samantha. Samantha's breath caught, and she turned into a Samantha log, as if an evil witch had suddenly frozen her.

Susie sniffed and backed away. Why was Samantha so mad at her?

"The tall, old ghost in the tall, old house wasn't a pretty ghost," Susie's mom read. "But he was a happy ghost. He was a very, very happy ghost."

Susie noticed her mom's eyes were shiny and wet. Susie also noticed her mom's voice sounded choked and crackly.

"Keep going," Samantha said.

Their mother sighed again.

Susie's mom returned to the familiar story about the ghost who was happy because he got to spend forever with his family . . . until he found out he wouldn't spend forever with them, since they were moving. That part always made Susie as sad as it made the ghost in the story. She couldn't imagine moving out of this house. Who would take care of Oliver?

Susie's mom read quickly, until she got to the part where the ghost found out that if he went away from the house, to a special place of sparkly light where the truly happy ghosts hung out, the ghost could never ever be separated from his family no matter where they went. She slowed down over that part, and she cleared her throat a lot.

Susie thought it would be very nice to be in a place where you'd never be separated from your family. She loved being with her mom and Samantha. Samantha could be a pain, but she *was* Susie's sister.

When the story was done, Susie's mom stood, hesitated, and went to the door. "Sleep sweet," she said.

Susie wished her mom would kiss and hug them goodnight like she used to. But Samantha had decided they were too old for that, and she wouldn't let her mom do that anymore. Apparently, her mom thought Susie agreed with Samantha—but she didn't.

As soon as her mom turned out the light, Samantha curled onto her side.

"Goodnight, Samantha," Susie said, but her sister didn't respond.

Susie shrugged and curled into a ball facing the window. She looked at the skinny curved piece of the moon that peeked into the room. Its light wasn't bright enough to see by, but it was bright enough to make a lot of funny shadows. Two of the shadows looked like dancing hippopotamuses, and three of them combined to look like a clown riding a horse. One of them looked a little like . . .

Susie closed her eyes. She listened to Samantha breathe, and she wondered if her sister had understood the drawings. Samantha hadn't said anything before she stuffed them under the covers. Why did she even put them there?

Outside, a dull thud sounded on the porch.

Already?

Susie didn't want to leave yet. She was hoping Samantha would take another look at the drawings. She just *had* to figure them out!

The thud was followed by a faint squeak—the sound of the porch swing moving. Then the thud turned into the footstep pattern Susie was so used to: *Thud . . . tap . . . thud . . . tap.*

Why did that sound make her skin crawl?

Why did she feel like she should know what was out there? Why did she feel like she *had* to know?

Susie pushed back the covers and got out of bed as if something was pulling her from its safety. It was like one of those tractor beams she'd seen in the space movies her dad liked to watch. She had no control. She wanted to stay in the nice warm bed. But instead, she walked out of the room and down the stairs.

At the bottom of the stairs she listened to the footsteps, and she watched a large shadow pass the dining room window. Once it passed, she trotted into the kitchen and opened the back door.

She waited.

Sometimes, Samantha would come and slam the back door, and they'd go back to bed. But not tonight.

Tonight, Susie could only stand there . . . listening to the footsteps come closer and closer. At the last minute, just before the steps came around the corner, she closed the kitchen door.

She tried to go back upstairs, but she couldn't. Instead, her feet took her to the entryway.

The house had a really big entryway, a "formal" entryway, her mom called it. She'd told Susie that, in the old days, there used to be a round table in the middle of the entryway. The table always held a vase full of flowers from the garden, but Susie's mom had put the table away when Susie's first walking had turned into wild running, because Susie kept bumping into the table and knocking off the vase.

"She broke seven vases before I gave up," Susie's mom liked to tell people. She never said it like she was mad. It seemed to make her happy for some reason.

Now the big entryway held only a maroon-and-navy-blue braided rug. Susie went to the middle of the rug and waited.

When the shadows shifted outside and the shape circling the house approached the front door, Susie stepped forward and opened it.

As Susie knew she would be, Chica stood tall and stiff outside the front door. The porch light played with Chica's yellow body, making it look like the animatronic was breathing. Susie looked up at Chica's pinkish-purplish eyes. Did Chica's big black eyebrows just move?

Susie looked down quickly. Chica's orange feet were planted on the WELCOME mat, one foot over the *W*, and one foot over the *M*. As always, Susie hesitated. But then she did as she knew she must. She held out her hand and let Chica enclose her stiff, cold fingers over her own.

Chica turned and walked toward the steps leading down to the leaf-covered front lawn. Susie had no choice but to go along. Now the small taps of her own footsteps joined with Chica's. And leaves crunched under their feet as they left Susie's house behind them.

In hushed stillness, Samantha listened to be sure her mother was in her room. She had to listen hard because the thick walls blocked little sounds. Eventually, though, she heard a creak she recognized as her mother's bed. She waited a few more minutes before turning on the flashlight under her covers and reaching for the drawings.

Samantha almost didn't need to see them. They'd been on her mind since the moment they appeared. In that time, she'd let herself admit that she knew the first picture was of her and Susie. But what did it mean?

Tenting her sheet and blanket, she aimed her flashlight at the drawing of the little girls.

At first, Samantha thought the flying-haired girl, Susie, held a mirror, but she quickly realized it was a magnifying glass. It looked like the one her dad used to have in his desk drawer in his office, the one he sometimes let the girls use to look at things up close. Samantha had never forgotten seeing Oliver's wood bark up close. It was like seeing a whole other world. Susie could name things all she wanted, but Samantha would rather study them. That's what she used the magnifying glass for—close-up study. Susie, though, used it to hunt.

After Susie used the glass to look at a caterpillar up close, she decided to use it to find "teeny-tiny" insects in the lawn. She was sure she was going to find something no one had ever seen before. When Samantha used the glass to look at Oliver's bark, Susie grabbed it and aimed it at a different part of his trunk. "Maybe we'll find some elves," she said.

Okay, so if Susie was holding a magnifying glass, she was looking for something.

But what? The floating baby?

Oh. No, not a baby. The floating thing was a doll.

Samantha frowned. If Susie was looking for a doll, there was only one doll missing.

It had to be Gretchen. So Susie wanted her back.

But what about the chick? What was that? Samantha didn't understand the toothy chick.

And what did the other drawing mean?

Samantha aimed her flashlight at the second drawing. It was just as she remembered: three panels with the flying-haired girl walking away from a door in the first two, just the door in the third, and moons that were a little bigger in each panel. What did that mean?

What if the moons getting bigger meant that each panel was a different day? Like tonight, tomorrow night, and the next night.

Samantha thought about her sister, the doll, and the moons.

She got it! Turning off the flashlight, she thought, *Susie's only going to be here for two more nights.*

She was pretty sure she had it right. But the chick... "What's the chick there for?" she whispered.

Susie, of course, didn't answer, because she was gone.

Samantha's alarm woke her before the sun came up. Thankfully, she was a light sleeper, so it didn't take much volume for her to hear it, and she was sure it wouldn't disturb her mom. Her mom had trouble going to sleep, but once she was asleep, she had just as much trouble waking up. Samantha had overheard her mom telling Jeanie that she could only sleep with the help of pills. The pills seemed to make mornings really hard, and Samantha had learned not to talk to her mom before school.

Once, Samantha had forgotten part of a school project. She and her mom were rushing around already because her mom had overslept. They had finally run out of the house and to the car, and her mom had driven only as far as the bottom of their driveway, when Samantha realized what she'd left behind in her room.

"I have to go back," she said.

Her mom hit the brakes so hard Samantha's head shot forward and back. She figured her mom would quickly drive back up to the house. Instead, her mom bent over and pounded her head several times on the steering wheel.

She whispered something over and over while she did it. Samantha thought it sounded like, "I can't do this."

Now Samantha laid in the dark, holding her alarm clock for several minutes. She didn't like getting up early. Susie had been the one who always wanted to hop out of bed and start playing before the sun was up. Susie was like their dad, who said the best part of the day was just before dawn when everything was in a "state of possibility."

"Smell that air," he'd say to Samantha on the few mornings he was able to talk her into getting up early. "Look at that pink light."

"It's so pretty," Susie would squeal.

Not pretty enough to get up early for, Samantha thought.

This morning, though, it wasn't the smell or the color that got Samantha out of bed. It was what she needed to do.

She only had two more days to find Gretchen.

She didn't know what would happen if she didn't find Gretchen. She didn't understand why a missing doll could mean so much to her dead sister. Susie was a ghost . . . wasn't she? Why would a ghost want something like a doll?

But it didn't matter. Susie wanted it, and after what had happened to her, she deserved to get what she wanted.

Samantha threw back the covers.

Cold air hit her bare legs, and goose bumps prickled her skin. She ignored her desire to dive back into bed. Instead she stood, letting the thick, soft material of her blue flannel nightgown block some of the cold air. She stuffed her feet into the leather moccasin slippers Jeanie had gotten for her

(Samantha didn't like fuzzy animal slippers like Susie did), grabbed the clothes she'd laid out during the night, and trotted into the bathroom on tiptoe.

Thankful for the little space heater that sat on a sturdy footstool by the bathroom door, Samantha turned it on and stood in front of it a couple minutes to warm up. Then she did a short version of her morning routine before getting dressed.

After she realized what Susie's drawings meant, Samantha had tried to stay awake long enough for her mom's pills to work so she could start looking for Gretchen. But she kept hearing her mom's bed creak, which meant her mom was not deeply asleep. Samantha's eyes had started to close, so she'd set her alarm for the morning.

When she finished in the bathroom, Samantha turned off the heater and opened the door. Stepping into the hallway, she stood on the dark-green braided runner and thought about where Susie might have hidden Gretchen.

Samantha glanced at Susie's closed door. She shook her head. The doll wouldn't be in there.

When Samantha and Susie had fought about Gretchen, Susie was as upset as she could possibly get. She wouldn't have put the doll in her room, where Samantha could easily find it. And even if it was in there, that was going to be the last place Samantha looked. She hadn't been in Susie's room since that horrible night when . . .

Samantha went down the hall toward the stairs. If she was going to look for the doll, she would do it in an organized way. It made sense to start at the bottom of the house and work up. Besides, on the first floor, there was less chance she'd wake her mom.

The porch light's pale yellow glow stretched up the stairs through the lead-glass window in the front door. The light was mottled and eerie.

"How can glass be lead?" Susie had asked when their dad told them what the glass in the door was called.

Samantha smiled now as she walked down the stairs. Susie was always asking questions like that. Samantha was never really sure if Susie was being funny or dumb.

At the bottom of the stairs, Samantha looked both ways. She could go either into the dining room or the living room. Besides the kitchen, the only other rooms on the first floor were a small bathroom and her dad's office. She doubted the doll would be in either of those rooms, because there weren't any hiding places in there.

She started in the dining room.

This dining room was at least double the size of any dining room Samantha had seen on TV. She couldn't really compare it with other people's dining rooms because she hadn't seen any others. She didn't have any friends. When Susie was alive, Samantha was sometimes invited to parties that Susie went to, but she stopped going after attending a couple. They were stupid and boring, and the kids were always mean to her.

Samantha wiped her forehead to brush away her memories. She turned on the wall switch so the light fixture over the table would come on low. The light was a big metal wheel with fake candles along its rim. Jeanie said the light fixture was "farmhouse style," which made sense.

"Why is it called a fixture?" Susie asked when they were little. "It doesn't fix anything."

Samantha crossed to the tall, carved hutch that sat behind one side of the long, dark dining table. She opened the lower doors. The hutch was full of china and crystal—dishes and glasses their family never used. She peered behind the stacks of plates and bowls. No Gretchen.

Moving on to the long low cabinet at the back of the room—the "sideboard," Jeanie called it—Samantha opened all the compartments and found lots of serving platters and vases. No Gretchen.

She went to the front of the room and opened the lid of the window seat. It was filled with tablecloths and napkins. Just to be sure, she dug under and between the stacks. No doll.

She went into the living room next. Outside, on the street, she heard the roar of the garbage truck emptying trash cans in front of all the houses. She chewed her lower lip. Would the garbage truck wake up her mom?

She'd better hurry.

The living room was big and filled with puffy, comfy furniture. It was too bad they hardly used it.

Samantha looked longingly at the long plaid sofa that faced the stone fireplace at one end of the room. Two solid burgundy loveseats joined the sofa to make a U shape.

Filled in at the corners with chunky oak end tables and centering around a square green ottoman, this was the place where the family used to play games by the fire.

At the other end of the living room was another big sofa, and a couple of recliner chairs faced a flat-screen TV. Sometimes, her mom would let Samantha watch that TV, but most of the time, she was supposed to watch shows on the computer in her room.

Around the edges of the room, built-in oak shelves and cabinets were stuffed with books and pictures in frames. Samantha remembered Susie's feelings about those shelves and some of the other furniture.

"Oak?!" Susie said one day when she was about six. "Oak, like Oliver?"

"Furniture is made from wood," their dad said, "and wood comes from trees."

"So they kill trees to make furniture?" Susie squealed.

Their parents had spent most of an hour trying to convince her the trees didn't feel pain when they were cut down. They never succeeded. Susie was sure the trees hurt.

Samantha started searching all the cabinets, beginning at the front corner and working clockwise around. When she didn't find anything, she felt behind all the books on the shelves. But she could only reach the bottom three rows.

She trotted into the kitchen pantry and got the stepladder that was kept in there. Defying her orderly plan, she searched the pantry while she was there. She found evidence that someone, other than her, had been hiding sweets: an old hardened bag of marshmallows, two half-eaten packages of chocolate chip cookies, an unopened box of old-fashioned donuts with a sell-it-by date that was a year ago, and a metal container of hard butterscotch candies that were all stuck together. But she didn't find Gretchen.

Dragging the stepladder back to the living room, she climbed up and down it fourteen times to look behind books and pictures. She found nothing but a lot of dust, which made her sad, because her mother used to want the house to be "spic-and-span." She remembered how the house used to smell like lemons from the spray her mom used when she dusted. Now, it just smelled like dust.

When she'd exhausted all the living room hiding spots, Samantha looked at the big wooden grandfather clock in the back hall. She had to get ready for school soon, and she had to wake her mom.

Before dragging the stepladder back into the kitchen, she peeked her head into the office. The only potential hiding place here was her dad's empty desk. She hurried in and opened all the drawers and looked in the cubbyhole where she'd once hung out by her dad's knees when she was really small. Nothing.

There was nothing to see in the entire room—just the desk and the empty shelves. The only other thing Samantha saw as she rushed from the room was a funny little piece of carpet stuck under the front edge of one of the shelves.

Risking a search of the kitchen before waking her mom, Samantha opened one cabinet and drawer after another, feeling behind dishes, pots and pans, plastic containers, baskets, and utensils. Gretchen remained hidden.

Samantha felt Susie's presence as soon as she got into the minivan after school that day. How did Susie do it? Samantha was sure Susie hadn't been around that morning, and she knew Susie was never in school.

Samantha ignored her sister's insistent presence and stared at the back of her mom's messy hair. Did her mom know Susie was here?

Samantha wondered if she should ask.

Maybe not while her mom was driving.

When her mom pulled into the driveway, Samantha turned to stare at Oliver, almost as if someone was making her do it. Usually, she ignored Oliver. Was Susie making her look? How?

Oliver only had a few leaves left. Maybe she'd come out and count them before dinner. No. She had to keep looking for Gretchen.

"Beans and franks for dinner?" her mom asked.

Something that felt like a wave flowed through Samantha. The wave was dark and kind of oily. It wanted to cling to Samantha the way sadness had clung to her since Susie was gone.

She thought the wave was emotion. But was it hers or Susie's?

Susie loved beans and franks. Was she sad that she couldn't have any? Did they have food where she'd gone when she died?

"Beans and franks are okay," Samantha said. "Can we have pineapple, too?"

In her mind, she saw Susie screw up her face in disgust. Did Susie put that image there? Samantha had always liked pineapple with beans, and Susie thought that was gross.

Their mom gave Samantha a half smile. "Sure."

Susie followed Samantha as she hurried from one room to the next in search of Gretchen. Samantha had been searching for Gretchen ever since they'd gotten home. Susie's drawings had worked!

Unfortunately, Samantha wasn't having any luck. This was partly because she was looking in dumb places.

For instance, Samantha had tried to find Gretchen in the hole in Oliver's tree trunk. Shining her light into the hole and muttering about elves, Samantha had held her breath and stuck her hand deep down inside the tree. Susie was laughing the whole time. Samantha had believed her when she'd talked about elves!

Now they were inside going all through the house. The sound of running water and clinking pans and silverware made it clear their mom was still in the kitchen. Obviously, Samantha was trying to search upstairs before their mom finished fixing dinner.

She started with their mom's studio.

"I would never have hidden Gretchen in here," Susie told Samantha when she opened the studio door. Samantha paid no attention to Susie. This wasn't a surprise; Samantha was being stubborn.

Why couldn't Susie remember where she put the doll?

She knew where she put it the first time she hid it. It had been in her room, under her bed, which she knew was a very unoriginal hiding place. A couple hours later, she'd moved it. But to where?

Susie stood in the doorway of her mom's studio while Samantha scurried around, digging in piles of fabric stacked on pale-yellow shelves, in mounds of yarn heaped in huge wicker baskets under a row of windows, and in canvas bins of wool sitting next to their mother's loom. Susie thought all of this was very brave because one of the standing house rules was that the studio was off-limits. Samantha even opened the door to the storage room on the far end of the studio. When she went in to search, Susie didn't follow.

Susie loved to play and be silly, but she wasn't crazy brave. The storage room held their mom's finished work, the stuff she sold to make money. They were never allowed to touch it. Once, when Susie was five, their mom had left one of her "tapestries" on the dining room table because someone was coming to pick it up. Curious, Susie went in the dining room, climbed up onto the chair, and looked at the tapestry. It was covered with fluffy tufts of soft round fabric that delighted her. She *had* to touch them. Forgetting she'd just eaten chocolate chip cookies, Susie put her sticky fingers all over the light-peach-colored tufts. When she saw the chocolatey smudges, she tried to wipe them off, which spread them around even more. This made her cry, and it scared her enough to try and run from the room. In her hurry, she ended up knocking over a chair and falling. Trying to catch herself, she grabbed the tapestry, and she still hit her head on the table, which made her shriek. When her mother ran into the room, Susie was on the floor with the chocolate-smeared tapestry in one hand, bleeding onto another part of the tapestry from a gash on her forehead.

Her mom had been *so* angry. It had scared Susie. It scared her so much she never went anywhere near her mother's work again.

Gretchen was not in her mother's studio. But Susie could only wait for Samantha to figure that out on her own.

Once she did, Samantha moved on to their mom's bedroom. First, she paused in the hallway to listen. More sounds from the kitchen encouraged Samantha to enter.

"Gretchen's not in here," Susie said as Samantha got down to peek under her mom's bed. The dark-blue bed skirt draped over Samantha's head like a scarf.

Samantha popped up off the floor, tilted her head to listen for a second, and then went into her mother's closet. Samantha began sweeping aside hanging clothes, opening and closing shoe boxes.

"Don't you think she would have found it by now if it was in here?" Susie said.

Samantha didn't answer.

Samantha looked up at the shelves above the hanging clothes. "You would just crawl up the racks," Samantha muttered.

Susie smiled. "Yes, I would."

Samantha turned in a circle, frowning. Spotting the bench that sat at the end of their mom's bed, Samantha dragged it into the closet.

Susie felt bad just standing there watching. But Samantha was wasting her time.

Samantha stood on the bench. Even on tiptoes, she had to strain to see the top shelves of her mom's closet.

Finishing with the closet, she moved to their mom's dresser. Susie chewed on her thumb. She was sure Samantha was going to get yelled at for what she was doing. Samantha had to know that, too, but she wasn't letting that stop her. Samantha searched through all of her mom's underwear, stockings, socks, and scarves.

"Samantha!"

"What?!" Samantha squealed, slamming shut the last dresser drawer.

"Dinner in five."

"Okay!"

Samantha ran to her mom's nightstand and searched it, then did the same with her dad's. His was empty. Her mom's was stuffed full of books, fabric samples, and pills. Gretchen was not hiding among them.

"I told you so," Susie said as she followed Samantha

from her mom's room. She knew she was being a snarky baby, but she couldn't help it. She could almost hear a ticking countdown in her head.

"Samantha has been snooping through my things," Patricia told Jeanie over the phone.

Discovering her materials had been rifled through, Patricia had decided to call her friend instead of yelling at her daughter.

"What things?"

"From what I can tell, all my things," Patricia said. She pressed three fingers to her temple. "Samantha knows better than that."

"Exactly. So she must have had a good reason," Jeanie said.

"What reason could she possibly have?"

"I don't know, but I know she had to have one. Nothing's missing or damaged?"

"Not that I can tell."

"Then let it go."

"But..."

"Seriously, Patricia. It's time to let it *all* go."

Chica came at midnight. As usual, Susie felt pulled from Samantha's bed. As usual, she felt compelled to wander around the house and watch Chica's dark shape circle outside. As usual, she opened the back door, then closed it and went to the front.

As usual, she wondered why she had to do what she had to do. Why did she have to leave her family?

Susie opened the front door, and the night breeze blew a couple of Oliver's leaves past Chica's feet and into the house. The night was brighter than the previous couple nights because the moon was fuller. The clouds were gone, too. Stars were so thick in the sky they reminded Susie of the powdered sugar her mom used to put on the chocolate crinkle cookies she made at Christmastime. In some places, the stars blurred into an expanse of brilliant white light.

Susie expected Chica to take her hand, as usual. Instead, Chica lifted a hand and pushed Susie aside. Then Chica walked into the house.

A nightmare woke up Samantha. Her eyes flew open, and she clutched her blankets, listening to her heart pound.

It was just a dream, she told herself. She felt her heart start to slow down.

Then it sped up again, and Samantha sat up.

It wasn't just a dream!

"Chica," she whispered.

Her dream had just told her more about the chick in Susie's drawing. The chick was Chica. Chica had been chasing Samantha in the dream. Samantha had been trying to move a shelf in her dad's office, and Chica had been stalking her.

Samantha gasped. Her dad's office! That's where . . .

Samantha froze when she heard sounds.

Thud . . . tap . . . thud . . . tap.

Samantha started to shake.

Those were the sounds. They were the same sounds Samantha had heard so many times over the last few months, the sounds she'd tried to convince herself she'd imagined.

She hadn't imagined them.

Those were the sounds.

Except they weren't exactly the same.

They were closer.

Much closer.

Samantha had always thought the sounds she'd heard came from outside the house. Now she knew they were inside, and coming closer.

When Chica started up the stairs, Susie tried to follow. But she couldn't. It was like she was glued to the doorway, trapped there by invisible chains.

"Chica, stop!" she yelled.

Chica didn't stop. She climbed slowly but steadily up the stairs.

She was going for Samantha; Susie was sure of it. Susie struggled to free herself from whatever held her in place. She tried and tried to move. Then she started to cry, and she did the only thing she could do to help her sister.

"Samantha!" she shouted. "Run!"

Samantha vaulted out of her bed and ran to her bedroom door. Could she get to her mom's room before whatever was coming up the stairs got to the top?

Opening her door a crack, she looked toward the stairs. No. It was too late. A bright yellow man-sized chick with horrible sharp teeth was one step from the top, just a few feet from Samantha's door.

She slammed her door and looked around her room. As the footsteps came closer, she dove under her bed.

When the door started opening, Samantha went rigid and held her breath as orange metal feet crossed the wood floor.

This couldn't be real.

But it was.

Trembling, Samantha watched the feet circle her bed. She couldn't hold her breath any longer, so she carefully let in a little air.

The feet stopped.

They turned.

They began coming back around the bed. Then they paused.

Samantha heard a terrifying whirring sound, and suddenly, the bedspread hanging over the side of the bed shifted. A yellow face with purplish eyes and deadly teeth peered at Samantha.

Samantha writhed away from the face, squirming toward the opposite side of the bed. Once out from under the bed, she looked over her shoulder, wondering if she could get past to flee her room before the chick straightened . . .

No. It was already standing, staring.

Samantha ran to the window. She tried not to listen to the *thud . . . tap . . . thud . . . tap* as she fumbled with the window lock.

Tremors, like butterfly wings, fluttered between her shoulder blades. She ignored them.

The steps muffled as they crossed her rug. She only had seconds.

Crawling through the window, Samantha gripped the interlocking diamonds of the trellis, and swung her legs out. The sound of ripping fabric made her look back through the window.

The chick was right there! It held a piece of her pale-blue nightgown in its hand.

Samantha whimpered and scrambled down the trellis. Keeping her gaze on the vine that clung to the trellis, she went as fast as she could. She was in her stocking feet, so the wood felt sharp against her soles, but she didn't care.

She also didn't look up. She didn't want to know if she was being chased.

When her feet encountered a rough, solid surface, she knew she'd reached the porch roof. Then she did look up.

Nothing was coming down the trellis after her. Good.

But not that good. If she wasn't fast enough, Chica could go back through the house and get her when she reached the porch.

Chica.

Samantha's mind had finally forced her to see what she hadn't wanted to see. The chick in the house was Chica.

In her drawing, Susie had been trying to say that Chica didn't want Susie to have Gretchen.

Why?

Samantha didn't know. But she knew she was right.

Chica was coming after her because she was looking for Gretchen.

Samantha gritted her teeth as she leaned over the edge of the porch roof to grab one of the porch posts. Could she grip it well enough to drop her legs down to the railing?

She had to. For Susie.

Samantha was going to get down and get back inside the house. Then she was going to find Gretchen... because thanks to her dream, she knew where to look.

But could she get there before Chica?

Susie didn't know how much time she was caught in the doorway listening to the sounds of Chica's footsteps upstairs. She heard several other thumps, too, but she never heard Samantha scream. She hoped that was a good sign, but she wasn't sure.

She thought she'd be in the doorway forever. Time went on and on and on.

Then she saw Chica at the top of the stairs. She was coming back down. And she didn't have Samantha.

If she could have moved, Susie would have fallen to the ground in relief. Instead, all she could do was watch Chica come down the steps.

Then, suddenly, Samantha appeared from outside!

Her face white and her eyes wide, her hair in a tangle, Samantha rushed past Susie.

Samantha's head was down, and her gaze was on her feet. She didn't look at Susie. She didn't even look up the stairs at Chica.

Susie watched Samantha dart into the dining room and disappear toward the kitchen. Where was Samantha going?

Samantha didn't know why she didn't think of it before. Maybe it was because, even though she kept thinking about him, she really wanted to forget her dad. It was bad enough that Susie got taken from them. At least Susie didn't leave on purpose. She didn't want to leave. She was taken, and she was *murdered*. *That*, Samantha thought, *is a pretty good excuse for leaving the family.*

Her dad, though, didn't have to leave. He left because it was "too hard." That was what he'd said. "It's too hard."

"But that's why we need you, Daddy," she'd said to him.

He'd just pressed his lips together—something she'd gotten from him—and said he had to go.

That's why Samantha was on her own now. Her dad was gone. Her mother was drugged asleep. Her sister was dead. If Samantha was going to survive, she'd have to save herself.

Even though Samantha didn't look up the stairs, she knew Chica was there. That's why she ran toward the kitchen.

She didn't know how smart Chica was, but she figured

it was worth trying to fool her. She wanted Chica to follow her into the kitchen and look for her there. If she'd judged right, it would give her enough time.

When she reached the kitchen, Samantha turned on the light. Then she tore through the back entrance of the kitchen and raced down the connecting hall to her dad's office.

In his office, she left the light off. She knew where she was going.

She ran to the shelf with the carpet piece. She grabbed the edge of the shelf at chest height, and she tugged on it. It didn't move. She bent over and tugged on the one below. No movement. The one above. Stuck. Stretching, she reached for the one above that. Still nothing.

It has to be! In her frustration, she kicked the shelf right next to the little carpet piece.

And the shelving unit popped free of the wall, opening out into the room. Susie had been right. A hidden room had been here all along.

Samantha didn't wait for the shelf-door to open all the way. She shouldered through the opening and groped for a light switch. She found one just inside the opening. Flipping the switch, she held still and listened.

She could hear Chica's footsteps in the kitchen. Good. It worked.

She looked around. The room was filled with all sorts of bizarre things—dried leaves, rocks, broken glass, old toys, stacks of papers and books. Samantha didn't know if she was looking at Susie's stash of treasures or her dad's. It didn't matter. It only mattered that Gretchen, her curly hair thick with dust but her polka-dot dress as bright as it was the day she disappeared, was sitting on top of one of the leaning book towers.

Samantha grabbed the doll and darted back through her dad's office. When she reached the doorway, she looked to her right. Chica was coming down the hall; she was only a few feet away.

Samantha fled through the living room and out through the front door. Panting, she looked out at the yard.

It was empty, of course. She knew where Susie was, and she knew where Chica was. Only Oliver stood in the yard—Oliver and his last pale-yellow leaf. Samantha ran to him, and hid behind his huge, solid trunk.

Susie watched Samantha hide behind Oliver, then she turned and waited for Chica to reach the entryway. What would Chica do? How could Susie keep Chica away from Samantha?

It turned out she didn't have to. When Chica reached Susie, Chica paused.

Chica held out a hand. Susie's hand raised and reached for Chica's even though that was the last thing she wanted it to do. She felt the animatronic metal touch her fingertips.

"But I'm not ready!" Susie told Chica.

Chica looked down, and her teeth gleamed in the moonlight. Susie shied back. Chica's fingers gripped Susie's tightly, and Susie couldn't pull them away. When Chica turned, Susie felt herself being dragged from her home. She knew she had to stop resisting. She had to go along.

So she stopped struggling, and she began calmly walking next to Chica.

Samantha watched Chica take her sister's hand, and she watched her sister and Chica cross the porch, come down the steps, and walk toward Oliver. Samantha tensed. What should she do? What *could* she do?

Before she could decide, Chica and Susie disappeared.

Not thinking, Samantha screamed, "Wait!"

Susie heard her sister's scream. Chica didn't pause, but Susie did. However much Chica was willing her to keep walking, something equally strong was willing her to go back. Caught in the middle, Susie, once again, couldn't move.

"Susie!" Samantha wailed her sister's name.

"I have to go back," Susie said. "I have to."

She waited, holding her breath. Then she felt something shift in the air around her.

Chica let go of her hand.

Samantha stepped out from behind Oliver and stood next to him, Gretchen dangling from her right hand. Tears filled her eyes.

She was too late.

No. What was that?

The leaves near Oliver's trunk swirled up from the ground and then out away from Oliver. The night was breezy, but the wind wasn't going in circles. It also was blowing toward Oliver, not away from him.

Samantha looked up at his sole surviving leaf again.

And that's when Susie suddenly appeared in front of Oliver.

She looked the same way she'd looked the day she was abducted. She even wore the same clothes—her magenta-and-pink striped sweater and the jeans Jeanie had studded with rhinestones.

Samantha stared at her sister. Then she held out Gretchen.

Susie opened her mouth like she wanted to say something. But then she just took the pudgy doll and clutched it to her chest.

"I've missed you so much," Samantha said.

Susie nodded. She reached out, and Samantha didn't even hesitate. She stepped into the offered hug.

Susie felt as solid as she had when she was alive. Maybe even more so. Samantha was never a hugger. She usually only half hugged Susie when Susie insisted on a hug. Now she hugged Susie with all of her strength. "I love you," she whispered.

She felt a wave of emotion flow over her, like the one she'd felt in the car. But this one wasn't dark and oily. This one was light, and it was warm and fizzy. Samantha was pretty sure this wave was a wave of love.

Susie let go, and Samantha brushed at the tears that ran down her cheeks. Susie smiled and then turned to Chica. Samantha watched Chica take her sister's hand. Then she watched Chica lead Susie, and Gretchen, away.

They disappeared just as Oliver dropped his last leaf.

"Goodbye," Samantha whispered.

Samantha felt the letting go. And she felt the promise of something new.

Susie was leaving, yes. But this wasn't an end. Samantha knew it was a beginning. Just like the happy ghost in the story, Susie was going where she could be with her family forever.

ABOUT THE AUTHORS

Scott Cawthon is the author of the bestselling video game series *Five Nights at Freddy's*, and while he is a game designer by trade, he is first and foremost a storyteller at heart. He is a graduate of the Art Institute of Houston and lives in Texas with his wife and four sons.

Andrea Rains Waggener is an author, novelist, ghostwriter, essayist, short story writer, screenwriter, copywriter, editor, poet, and a proud member of Kevin Anderson & Associates' team of writers. In a past she prefers not to remember much, she was a claims adjuster, JCPenney's catalog order-taker (before computers!), appellate court clerk, legal writing instructor, and lawyer. Writing in genres that vary from her chick-lit novel, *Alternate Beauty*, to her dog how-to book, *Dog Parenting*, to her self-help book, *Healthy, Wealthy, & Wise*, to ghostwritten memoirs to ghostwritten YA, horror, mystery, and mainstream fiction projects, Andrea still manages to find time to watch the rain and obsess over her dog and her knitting, art, and music projects. She lives with her husband and said dog on the Washington Coast, and if she isn't at home creating something, she can be found walking on the beach.

Elley Cooper writes fiction for young adults and adults. She has always loved horror and is grateful to Scott Cawthon for letting her spend time in his dark and twisted universe. Elley lives in Tennessee with her family and many spoiled pets and can often be found writing books with Kevin Anderson & Associates.

Kelly Parra is the author of YA novels *Graffiti Girl, Invisible Touch*, and other supernatural short stories. In addition to her independent works, Kelly works with Kevin Anderson & Associates on a variety of projects. She resides in Central Coast, California, with her husband and two children.

Jake looked down at himself and tried to get used to the fact that "himself" wasn't anything like the himself he'd been used to being before. Last he could remember, he'd been a little boy. He hadn't been a boy in a while . . . he didn't know how long.

So it wasn't totally weird that he wasn't in a little boy's body anymore. But it was still pretty weird that he was in a thing that wasn't alive. It was also weird that he couldn't remember exactly who he'd been when he was a little boy. He had vague bits of memories, but they didn't make sense. Like, he could remember thinking it would be fun to come back to life as a puppy or a kitten. But why would he think that?

Now here he was inside a metal thing. He didn't know enough about anything to understand what it was. But he did know he wasn't alone. He was sharing this strange space.

It was like waking up in in another family's house.

"Hello?" Jake said.

"Who's talking?" a child's voice asked. The child sounded a little like a boy Jake used to know in school, a boy who was always talking back to the teacher and getting himself in trouble.

"Oh, hi," Jake said. "I'm Jake. Who're you?"

"What's it to you?"

"Um, I was just being friendly."

Jake remembered learning that the way to deal with kids like this was to let them be as tough as they wanted to be.

"Sorry. I'm Andrew." The child's voice was rough. He didn't sound like he was saying his name. It sounded like he was throwing down a challenge.

"Hi, Andrew," Jake said.

"Why can't I see anything?" Andrew demanded.

"You can't see the truck?" Jake asked.

"If I could see the truck, do you think I'd say I can't see anything?"

Jake thought Andrew sounded angry. Very angry.

"Sorry," Jake said. "Um, so we're in the back of what I think might be a trash truck? We're with a lot of junk."

"Figures," Andrew said.

"How come?" Jake asked.

"Story of my life."

"What do you mean?"

Andrew ignored the question. "How come you can see

and I can't?" He sounded like he was gearing up for a tantrum.

"I'm really sorry. I'm not sure," Jake said. "I mean, I know we're in some kind of metal thing, I don't know, some kind of entity or something? I can see what's around it, but I don't know how I got here, and so I don't know how *you* got here. And I sure don't know why I can see and you can't. But maybe I can help you see. Do you know how you got here?"

Andrew was silent for a minute. Jake waited.

"Well, it might have had something to do with the stuff I was in?"

"What stuff?" Jake asked.

"How is it any of your business?" Andrew snarled.

Jake sighed. "It's not. I just thought it would be nice to be friends, and friends get to know each other. So I just wondered what you meant by being *in stuff*."

The truck ground to a stop, and there was silence.

"I haven't had a friend in a long time," Andrew said. His tone was defensive, as if he was daring Jake to make fun of him.

"I'm so sorry," Jake said. His memories were disjointed and muddled, but he remembered he'd had friends. "That's awful."

Jake wanted to know more, but he knew better than to keep asking questions.

The back of the truck opened, and a guy in coveralls started unloading all the junk. "I could be your friend," Jake said.

"Why would you want to be my friend?"

"I just like making friends," Jake said.

"So how do we do that?"

"Do what?"

"Make friends!" Andrew made an exasperated puffing sound. "Geez, you're dense."

Jake felt like he was making first contact with a new species, like in sci-fi movies he could remember watching.

"We talk to each other, tell each other things and find out about each other, and then we become friends," Jake said. He figured that was close enough.

"Like what things?" Andrew asked.

"Whatever you want." Jake wanted to ask again about what Andrew meant by being *in stuff*, but he waited.

Andrew was silent for a few seconds. "Have you ever been so angry you just wanted everyone to know it?"

Jake thought about it and remembered a time he was really angry because he had to leave school. But why? It didn't matter.

"I've been really angry," he said, "but I guess I didn't need everyone to know it. But I had someone to talk to. Did you?"

"No."

Jake wasn't sure what to say, so he stayed quiet.

"Did you want to get back at the person you were angry with?" Andrew asked.

"I don't think it was a person. I think it had to do with

being sick or something. My memories are kind of fuzzy."

"Fuzzy. Yeah. So are mine," Andrew said. "But I do remembering wanting to get back at someone who hurt me. I think I attached myself to him. I got into his soul, made sure he couldn't move on when he shoulda died. I remember I wanted him to suffer, the way he made me suffer. But I don't remember what he did. I just know I hung on, no matter what they did to him to try and save him. I wanted him to *hurt*!"

At one point, Jake couldn't hold back any longer. He blurted, "That's terrible that you felt so bad."

"Shut up. Just shut up," Andrew yelled. "I don't need your stupid sympathy!"

"Sorry."

Several seconds passed.

Then Andrew had more to say. "I remember they tried to kill him. But I wasn't going to let him go until I was ready. It's weird. I remember being so angry and determined, but I don't know why."

It hurt Jake to be so close to this much hate. But he wouldn't have left if he could have. Andrew needed him.

"You still there?" Andrew asked Jake.

"Yes. I'm listening. You told me to shut up."

Andrew laughed. "Yeah, I did, didn't I?"

Jake was quiet. Then he said, "So where is the person now, the one you're angry with?"

"I'm not sure. I know I was in him when we got to this big place with lots of cool stuff. All I can remember after that is wanting to be everywhere. I can remember being all over the place in all kinds of things. And I remember this animatronic dog, Fetch. He broke down in a thunderstorm. Sucky toy. Not made well." Andrew made a raspberry sound. Then he sighed. "So I think I was in Fetch, sort of. I think that's how I got here. I don't know why I think that. I just do."

Jake stayed silent. He was still watching the man unload the truck.

"You can talk now," Andrew said.

"I don't know what to say," Jake said. "I feel bad that you went through something that was really bad."

The man reached for Jake and Andrew's container. Jake had been wondering what to do about the man. He thought moving what they were in would startle the man. But now he didn't really have a choice. He didn't want the man to throw Andrew and him away.

So Jake moved, which meant the thing they were in moved. Jake saw the man stare in alarm. Wanting to comfort the man, Jake reached out to touch his face.

The man screamed and grabbed his head. Collapsing on the gravel behind the truck, the man's body began to wither like he was a sponge being wrung out by an invisible hand. As his body sucked in on itself, his eyes fell inward, disappearing. And black streaks ran down the man's cheeks.

"What just happened?" Jake shouted. He jumped out of the truck and stared at the bald man's body.

"I can't see, dummy," Andrew snapped. "What are you talking about?"

"I just thought about touching a guy's face, and he died! Why'd he die?!" Jake realized he was screaming, but he couldn't help himself.

"Why're you asking me?" Andrew was sounding defensive again.

"The other guy died, too. I just remembered," Jake said.

"It's probably me," Andrew said.

"Could it be Fetch, the dog?" Jake asked.

"Nah, it's me, I bet."

"You want to kill people?"

"No!"

"Then why . . . ?"

"I just want to scare people, okay? Like, you know, give them a zap."

"The zap is killing them!"

"Well, that wasn't what I wanted."

"Okay." Jake thought a second. "So if what you're doing isn't doing what you want, maybe it's doing something someone else wants. Maybe something else is here with us."

"In this thing, you mean?"

"Yeah. Like a hitchhiker or like a flea on a dog."

"That's stupid," Andrew said.

"You were a hitchhiker on the man who killed you. Why can't someone else hitchhike with us?"

Andrew was silent for second, then he said, "It just sounds dumb."

"The thing is," Jake said, "that if you did do it somehow, whatever is causing you to do it could be in everything you got into."

"I infected them. I remember now."

"What?"

"I infected everything I threw my anger at."

"Okay. So everything you infected could hurt people. Innocent people."

"Hey, I'm not like that. I just wanted to hurt the bad guy."

"But you said you infected stuff with your anger. You didn't think that would hurt them?"

"Shut up."

"Fine, I'll shut up. But we're going to go find all the stuff you infected."

"How're you gonna do that?"

"You won't help me?"

"Why should I?"

Jake thought for a second and then tried something. He wasn't sure he could do it. But . . .

Yes, he could! He could feel Andrew's thoughts. He'd be able to find the stuff Andrew infected, even without Andrew's help.